1 DINOSAUR DETECTIVE

On the Right Track

—To DML

Book design by Debora Smith

Scientific American Books for Young Readers is an imprint of W. H. Freeman and Company, 41 Madison Avenue
New York, New York 10010

Library of Congress Cataloging-in-Publication Data

Calhoun, B. B.

On the right track / by B. B. Calhoun

—(Dinosaur detective ; #1)

Summary: Fenton Rumplemayer moves from New York City to Wyoming with his father, a paleontologist, and is able to help him identify a puzzling dinosaur track.

ISBN 0-7167-6519-5 (hard). —ISBN 0-7167-6530-6 (soft)

[1. Dinosaurs—Fiction. 2. Paleontology—Fiction. 3. Mystery and detective stories.]
I. Title. II. Series: Calhoun, B. B. Dinosaur detective ; #1.

PZ7.L9649On 1994

[Fic]—dc20 93-37745
CIP
AC

Printed in the United States of America.

10 9 8 7 6 5 4 3 2 1

1 DINOSAUR DETECTIVE

On the Right Track

B. B. Calhoun

illustrated by Daniel Mark Duffy

W.H. FREEMAN AND COMPANY NEW YORK

1

Fenton Rumplemayer walked through the doors of the New York Museum of Natural History and waved to the guard near the front desk. Everyone at the museum knew Fenton. His parents worked there as paleontologists, scientists who study dinosaur bones and try to put them together. Fenton had been visiting the museum for about as long as he could remember.

He had spent many hours there sketching dinosaur skeletons in his special notebooks, and he knew every dinosaur in the museum by heart. Today was the last day of school, and Fenton was looking forward to spending the long, hot summer days sketching in the cool, dark dinosaur halls. As far as Fenton was concerned, the museum was the best place in the world. He had even already decided what he was going to be when he grew up—the world's biggest expert on dinosaurs.

Fenton knew he had to stop by the lab and let his parents know he was there before going to see the dinosaurs. Making his way past the museum gift shop and through the meteorite display room, he climbed the stairs to the second floor. He pushed open the heavy door that said PRIVATE—MUSEUM STAFF ONLY and found his mother and father sitting together at a worktable, bending over a pile of small bones.

"Hi, Mom. Hi, Dad," said Fenton, walking up to the table and dropping his stegosaurus backpack on the floor. "Hey, what's that?"

"Hello, Fenton," said Anne Rumplemayer, setting down the small bone she was holding and reaching toward her son for a quick hug. "How was your last day of school?"

Fenton was busy looking at the bones on the table.

"That's going to be a hand, isn't it?" he asked, pointing at a few of the bones that had already been assembled. "What kind of dinosaur is it from?"

Fenton's father looked up from the two tiny bones he was examining.

"Oh, hello, son," he said. "These just arrived from a dig site in Colorado. Aren't they something? It looks like we might have a complete hand here, all right."

"We're pretty sure it's the hand of a camptosaurus," explained Fenton's mother.

Fenton nodded. He knew that the camptosaurus was a medium-sized, plant-eating dinosaur that usually walked on two feet. "See this pointed piece here?" asked his mother, indicating a sharp, triangular, spiky-looking bone. "This is its thumb."

"Camptosaurus probably used this as a weapon to fight off attacking dinosaurs," explained his father.

Fenton examined the bone. It definitely looked sharp enough to wound another dinosaur pretty badly. He remembered the complete camptosaurus skeleton the museum had on display on the third floor.

"I think I'll go upstairs and make some sketches," he said, picking up his backpack.

"All right, Fenton, but make sure you're back here in an hour so we can go home," Mrs. Rumplemayer called after him.

But Fenton was already out the door and hurrying up the stairs. When he got to the third floor, he walked straight through the Hall of the Late Mammals and the Hall of the Early Mammals to the Hall of the Late Dinosaurs.

The Hall of the Late Dinosaurs was filled with fossils from the end of the Age of Dinosaurs, the Cretaceous Period, which began 145 million years ago and ended when the dinosaurs disappeared about 65 million years ago.

Fenton easily found the camptosaurus skeleton on its pedestal on the far side of the room. Pulling his sketchbook and his box of colored pencils out of his backpack, he settled himself on the floor in front of the giant skeleton.

As usual, he began by sketching the bones. After he had the skeleton down on paper, it would be easier to imagine what the dinosaur had looked like when it was alive. Paying special attention to the spiked thumb, Fenton sketched the bones of the camptosaurus onto the sheet of paper in front of him.

Next he filled in the flesh over the bones. As far as Fenton was concerned, one of the most interesting things about drawing dinosaurs was that no one knew for sure exactly what color they were. He decided to make his camptosaurus green and brown.

The camptosaurus was standing on its hind legs. Fenton drew a tall green plant for it to nibble at and added some rocks and other plants.

Now maybe he should give the camptosaurus a chance to use its thumb spike. For that, Fenton would have to create a fight between the camptosaurus and another dinosaur. He looked around and saw the skeleton of an allosaurus, a large, meat-eating dinosaur, nearby. Allosaurus was a good choice because it lived at the same time as camptosaurus. He decided to add the allosaurus in the background of the drawing, getting ready to attack the camptosaurus.

Flipping the page of his sketchbook, Fenton drew the allosaurus getting closer to the unsuspecting camptosaurus. In the next sketch, the camptosaurus spotted the allosaurus and reared up, thumb spikes extended. The allosaurus opened its mouth, exposing its terrible teeth, but the camptosaurus was ready to strike with its thumb spike.

Then Fenton heard a voice from directly above him.

"Fenton Rumplemayer, do you know what time it is?"

Fenton looked up and saw his mother standing in the doorway with her hands on her hips.

"Don't you remember my telling you to meet me back at the lab in an hour?" she asked. She sighed, shaking her head. "Come on, it's time for us to go."

"Aw, Mom," said Fenton, "I'm not finished yet."

"Well, I'm sorry, but you'll just have to finish another time," she said. "I want to get home and get dinner started."

Fenton closed his sketchbook reluctantly. Now he might never know how the battle between the camptosaurus and the allosaurus would have turned out. He'd tried working on his dinosaur sketches at home, but somehow they never came out the way they did at the museum.

Mr. Rumplemayer had gone to drop some books off at the library nearby, so Fenton and his mother left the museum and headed across the street to their apartment building.

Gus, the doorman, let them into the lobby.

"Hello there, Fenton," he said with a wink. "Special delivery letter came for you today, Mrs. Rumplemayer."

"Really?" said Fenton's mother, sounding surprised. "Thanks, Gus." She took the envelope from him and began to open it as Fenton ran ahead to press the button for the elevator.

"Come on, Mom, I've got it," called Fenton, holding down the DOOR OPEN button. What was taking her so long?

Mrs. Rumplemayer walked slowly into the elevator, her eyes on the piece of paper in her hand.

"What is it, Mom?" asked Fenton, pushing the button for the twelfth floor.

"It looks like I've received a grant," his mother said slowly, her eyes still on the letter in her hands.

"You mean like a grant of money?" asked Fenton.

"Yes," said his mother, looking up. "It's a research grant, for fieldwork, digging dinosaurs in India for a year."

"What are you talking about?" asked Fenton as the elevator opened. He followed his mother down the hall toward their apartment. "You mean *going* to India?"

"Well, yes," said Mrs. Rumplemayer, digging in her purse for the keys. "If I decide to accept it, that is."

"What do you mean, *if!*" said Fenton excitedly. How could his mother think of letting the family miss out on a chance like this? "I mean, India, wow, that sounds really cool!"

"Now hold on, Fenton," said his mother, putting her key in the lock and turning to face him. "Let's not get all worked up about this right away. There are a lot of things to figure out. And I need to talk to your father before I make any decisions."

"Okay, okay," said Fenton. "But can I go down to Max's?"

Max was Fenton's best friend. They lived in the same apartment building and were in the same class at school.

"Oh, all right," said his mother, "but make sure you're back up here in half an hour for dinner. And this time I mean half an hour."

"Sure thing, Mom!" Fenton said quickly, handing her his backpack and hurrying back down the hall to the staircase so he wouldn't have to waste a moment waiting for the elevator.

India, imagine! Wait until Max heard this! Until now, the farthest places Fenton had ever been were Florida and California. And now he was practically going to the other side of the world! He wondered if he'd see any wild tigers there. Hadn't he heard that wild tigers roamed the countryside in India?

Fenton was so excited by the time he got down to the ninth floor that he rang Max's doorbell six times.

Max's father answered the door with an exasperated look on his face.

"Oh, Fenton, it's you," he said.

"Hi, Mr. Bellman, I have to see Max right away, it's very important," Fenton said in one quick breath, brushing past him and heading down the hall to Max's room.

He threw open the door and found Max sitting at his desk in front of his computer. Max was practically a computer genius. He knew more about computers than anyone Fenton had ever met. Max had even created his own computer game, called Treasure Quest.

"Max, wait till you hear this—" cried Fenton, still out of breath.

"Fenton, you're here! Great!" said Max, looking up from the screen in front of him. "You're just in time to try level four of Treasure Quest. I just finished designing it, and it's really cool. You see, after you get your explorer through the caves on level three—"

"Hold on, Max," Fenton cut him off. "I have something really incredible to tell you."

Max looked at him. "Fenton, didn't you hear what I said? There's a whole new level of Treasure Quest! Come on, let's try it out!"

"But this is something even more important," Fenton said.

Max stared at him. Fenton knew what Max must be thinking—what could be more important than a new level of Treasure Quest? But just wait until Max heard this news.

Fenton took a deep breath.

"I, Fenton Rumplemayer," he began, "am about to set off on an adventure as exciting as *anything* in Treasure Quest."

"Fenton," Max sighed, "what are you talking about?"

Fenton cleared his throat. He didn't like to be rushed, especially when he had something this exciting to say.

"Max," he announced solemnly, "I am going to India."

"India? Fenton, what do you mean?" asked Max. "Oh, I get it—is this some kind of nutty way of telling me about an India exhibit that's coming to the museum or something?"

"No, really!" said Fenton. "I'm actually going to India! My mother got a grant to study dinosaur bones there for a year.

She just found out about it today."

Max's mouth dropped open a little, but nothing came out.

"Isn't that great?" asked Fenton excitedly. "I mean, I was thinking, they probably have tigers there and everything. And elephants—maybe I'll even get to ride an elephant."

"Hold on, Fenton," said Max. "Are you trying to tell me that your whole family's just going to pick up and go to India? Just like that?"

Fenton nodded.

Max was silent for a moment, and it began to seem to Fenton like Max was a lot less excited about the news than Fenton had expected.

"What about your father?" Max asked suddenly. "Doesn't he still have to go to his job at the museum?"

Fenton paused. He didn't really want to admit that he had been so thrilled with the idea of going to India that he hadn't thought about that part of it before.

"Well, maybe he'll get a new job there or something," he said, shrugging.

But he couldn't help wondering—would his father really quit his job at the museum? The grant was only for his mother, wasn't it? What kind of job would his father be able to get in India?

Just then Fenton heard the click of Max's computer mouse. He looked over and saw Max peering intently at the screen. He couldn't believe it. He had just told Max the most exciting news of his life, and Max seemed more interested in his computer.

"So, Max," Fenton said enthusiastically, "isn't that great news?"

Max shrugged and continued fiddling with the mouse.

Fenton was confused. Why wasn't Max saying anything?

"Max, are you even listening to me?" he asked.

"Yes, Fenton, I heard you," said Max, without looking up. "So you're going to India on a big adventure. Great. But right now I have to do some important work on level four of Treasure Quest, if you don't mind."

"I thought you said you had finished level four when I came in," Fenton pointed out. "Besides, isn't what I'm talking about more important? After all, this is going to be a real-life adventure. Treasure Quest is just a computer game."

Max turned to face him, his face bright red.

"Listen, Fenton," he yelled, "maybe Treasure Quest isn't that important to you anymore, but it's still important to me! And this new level I've designed isn't exactly easy, you know. It's going to take a lot of practice to master level four—a lot. But I guess that doesn't really matter to *you,* since you're not even going to be around to play it!"

Fenton was shocked. He had never heard Max yell that way before. He didn't know what to say.

"Hey, come on, Max," he tried.

But Max just stared angrily down at the computer in front of him and refused to answer.

Fenton didn't know what to do. He looked around the room and tried to think of something to say.

Suddenly he noticed the digital clock next to Max's bed. He was already five minutes late for dinner! He knew his mother was going to be pretty upset if he didn't get moving.

He looked at Max one more time, but Max was still staring at his computer and ignoring him. Silently Fenton turned and left the room.

Having Max yell at him like that had taken away some of Fenton's good mood, so on the way down the hall to the elevator, he did his best to get excited about India again. He tried to imagine what it would be like there. Where would his family live? Did they have apartments in India? As he pressed the button for the elevator, he thought about what it would be like to live somewhere else. It made him feel kind of strange. After all, he had lived in this apartment building his whole life.

Suddenly Fenton realized what it was that had made Max so upset. If Fenton went to India, that meant that he and Max wouldn't see each other for a whole year! It gave Fenton a funny feeling in his stomach to think about it.

As Fenton got off the elevator on the twelfth floor, he forced himself to think about the tigers and the elephants, and before he knew it, the funny feeling was almost completely gone. After all, he and Max could still write to each other, couldn't they? Not that Fenton had ever been very good at writing letters. But maybe his parents would let him call Max from India sometimes. Sure, he and Max would miss each other, but the important thing to remember was that Fenton was going on the adventure of his life.

As he let himself in the front door, he heard his parents' voices coming from the kitchen. That was kind of strange. Usually his father worked at his desk in the living room before dinner.

Fenton went into the kitchen and found his mother stirring a big pot and his father leaning against the refrigerator. As soon as they saw him, they stopped talking. Fenton noticed the special-delivery letter on the counter between them.

"What's going on?" he asked, opening the refrigerator and peering inside.

"Don't eat anything," said his mother. "Dinner will be ready in just a minute."

Fenton sniffed—mmm, spaghetti, his favorite.

"Besides," said his father, "we'd like to talk to you about something, son."

Fenton closed the refrigerator.

"Okay," said Fenton, starting to feel kind of excited. India, here I come, he thought.

"Your father and I have just been talking things over," his mother explained. "And we have a few things to tell you." She glanced over at Fenton's father. "First of all, I've decided to accept the grant to go to India."

"All right!" cheered Fenton.

"Well, I'm glad you're so happy for me, Fenton," said his mother, pouring the boiling water from the spaghetti into the sink. "It wasn't an easy decision to make. And of course it will be very hard for me to be away from you and your father for that long. But I've decided that it's a chance I just can't pass up. There are several dinosaur species I'm interested in studying that appear only in India."

Fenton shook his head. What was she talking about?

"A year will go faster than we all think," his father put in. "Before we know it, we'll all be together again."

Fenton couldn't believe his ears. Were his parents trying to tell him that his mother was going to India alone?

"Wait a minute! You mean Dad and I have to stay in here New York?" he cried.

His father smiled. "Well, not exactly, son. That's the other thing we have to tell you. You and I are going to take off on a little adventure of our own."

"Your father has decided to accept a job as the head of a team of paleontologists in Wyoming," explained his mother.

"Wyoming State University has been working on a pretty big dig site out there, and the museum's been trying for quite a while to get me to go and head the team," said Mr. Rumplemayer. "Now that your mother will be spending some time out of the country, it seems like the perfect opportunity."

Fenton looked wildly from his mother to his father. Could they be serious?

"You mean I'm *not* going to India?" he asked.

His mother looked at him, the big bowl of spaghetti in her hands and a sympathetic look on her face.

"Oh, no, honey," she said. "You couldn't possibly come with me. I'm going to be traveling around to small villages quite a bit, and spending a lot of time out in the field. Why, how would you go to school? In Morgan, you'll go to the local school, and I'm sure you'll make lots of new friends. Now come sit at the table, dinner's ready."

"Morgan?" Fenton repeated faintly, trailing into the dining room behind his parents.

"Morgan, Wyoming," his father said cheerfully as he sat down at the table. "It's in the southern part of the state, not too far from the Colorado border. Beautiful country out there. I did some work in that area when I was still in college. . . ."

Fenton sank into his chair, no longer hearing anything his father was saying. He felt numb. He certainly didn't care about where in Wyoming this Morgan place was. Why, Fenton didn't even really know where Wyoming was.

One thing Fenton did know for sure, though. If he couldn't go to India, there was no way he wanted to leave New York City, and the museum, and his school, and Max, and Treasure Quest—especially not for someplace he had never even heard of.

2

"Well, I guess I'd better head over to the museum," said Fenton's father one evening two weeks later. "I still have to pick up some things to take on the plane to Morgan tomorrow."

"Can I go, too, Dad?" asked Fenton. He loved being in the museum after hours. Besides, he thought, this will be my last chance to see the dinosaurs for a whole year.

Fenton still couldn't believe that this was going to be their last night in New York, that the next morning his mother would leave for India and he and his father would fly to Wyoming.

Ever since he had found out that he wasn't going to India after all, Fenton's mood had been as glum as Max's. The first thing Fenton had done the morning after his parents had told him about Wyoming was to go talk to Max. The two boys had made up easily, but neither of them had been very happy with the idea that they would have to spend a whole year apart.

What made it even worse for Fenton was the way everyone else expected him to be excited about the move. His mother kept saying it would be beautiful in Wyoming, and his father talked about all the fresh air they would be breathing. Even Gus the doorman had something to say, telling Fenton how lucky he'd be to be able to live in a real house where he could play outside. No one seemed to understand that Fenton didn't *want* to live in a house and breathe fresh air. He *liked* living in his apartment across from the Museum. And he didn't care about playing outside. He'd much rather stay inside and draw dinosaurs or play Treasure Quest with Max.

"Maybe I'll take a walk over to the museum with you two," said Fenton's mother. "After all, I don't have too many hours left to spend with my boys." Her eyes looked misty.

Fenton turned his head the other way. He didn't like to think about how it was going to be to have his mother so far away. She had promised to write him a lot, and to call whenever she could, but the whole idea still made him feel kind of funny inside.

Fenton and his parents walked across the street to the museum and rang the night bell by the staff entrance. A guard came to the door to let them in, and the Rumplemayers headed up to the second floor.

"Can I go to the dinosaur halls?" asked Fenton.

"Just for a few minutes," said his mother. "You're not really supposed to be up there when the museum is closed."

Fenton took the stairs two at a time to the third floor. Most of the lights were off, but Fenton knew his way around so well that he probably could have done it with his eyes closed.

The skeletons in the Hall of the Early Dinosaurs loomed huge and dark against the red glow of the exit lights. There was the dilophosaurus, with the strange double-crest on its skull. And the coelophysis with its long, delicate neck and tail. Fenton walked slowly around the center display area, his hand trailing on the low metal railing. He knew these dinosaurs so well that they seemed like old friends.

He thought of a story his mother sometimes told. When Fenton was only about four years old, his parents had brought him to work with them at the museum. Fenton's father was supposed to be keeping an eye on him while his mother was at a meeting. But Mr. Rumplemayer got involved in examining a new skull that had just come in, and somehow Fenton managed to wander out the door of the lab. His parents were frantic when they realized he was missing—they had practically the whole museum searching for him. Finally a guard found him right there in the Hall of the Early Dinosaurs, lying on the floor and gazing up at the coelophysis.

Fenton sighed. It was probably time to go back down to his parents. He walked toward the door of the room, turning to glance back at the giant creatures one more time.

Downstairs he found his parents in their office, a little room off their lab. It looked strange to see the office so empty. For as long as Fenton could remember, it had been crowded, its two big desks covered with books, papers, and even bones. There had been pictures and diagrams all over the walls, including some of Fenton's own drawings. Fenton wondered when he would ever draw dinosaurs again. Sure, it was possible that he would see a few bones at the dig site where his father was supposed to work in Wyoming, but Fenton was certain that whatever he might see there couldn't possibly compare to drawing all of those fully assembled skeletons in the museum.

Fenton's mother was taping shut a cardboard box while his father closed a squarish plastic suitcase.

"What's all that stuff?" asked Fenton.

"Equipment for my office in Morgan," said his father. "The museum is letting me take the computer and FAX machine from here so I can use them for my work out there."

"This FAX machine can receive a letter in a few seconds," said Fenton's mother, applying a last bit of tape to the box. "That means that if I'm near a FAX machine, too, I can send you a FAX from India and you'll get the letter right away."

"Cool," said Fenton. He liked the idea of being able to read a letter from his mother moments after she had written it. Then he thought of something. "I'll have to wait for Dad to bring it home from work, though, first."

"Oh, we'll probably set up the FAX machine at home, son," said Fenton's father, lifting a box of files under one arm and gripping the suitcase in his other hand. "I don't think I'll have much of an office out at the dig site. Maybe some space in a tent or a trailer, but certainly nothing with enough power for a lot of office equipment. I'll probably just take my own lap-top computer to the dig site and then set up a study in our house somewhere with the FAX and the desk-top computer." He looked at Fenton and smiled. "Oh, and here's something you might be interested in, son." He held up the plastic case. "This desk-top computer has a built-in modem."

"You mean it can hook up by a telephone line to another computer?" asked Fenton.

"That's right," said his father. "I suppose you and Max might want to keep in touch that way."

"Wow!" said Fenton happily. A computer with a built-in modem! This was great news—now he and Max could send each other messages, and even play Treasure Quest.

"Ready to go, Anne?" asked Fenton's father.

"Sure, Bill," said Fenton's mother, lifting the box with the FAX machine. "Here, Fenton, why don't you carry this."

She handed him a small, heavy object that he recognized as the paperweight from her desk. The clear glass dome held a tiny replica of a dinosaur egg. One side of the egg was cracked, and a baby dinosaur could be seen pushing its way out. It wasn't real, but it was an exact miniature copy of a maiasaur, a member of the hadrosaurid or "duckbill" family of dinosaurs. Baby maiasaurs were only inches long, but they could grow to over twenty feet. Fenton knew that maiasaurs laid their eggs in giant nests and that they fed and took care of their babies until the young dinosaurs could look after themselves.

He put the paperweight in the pocket of his jean jacket and

followed his parents down the stairs and out into the breezy New York night.

It was pretty late by the time they got back to the apartment, but Fenton knew he had to call Max and tell him the news about the modem.

"Cool," said Max. "Let's play Treasure Quest tomorrow."

"Okay," said Fenton. "I'll contact you tomorrow night on the modem from Morgan."

"All right," said Max. "Modem me at eight-thirty. I'll be at my computer here in New York waiting."

"Eight-thirty P.M. sharp," agreed Fenton.

"Hey, Fenton," said Max, as they were about to hang up.

"What, Max?"

"Now it can be almost like you never left New York at all."

"Yeah," said Fenton. That's what he was hoping, too.

3

Fenton pressed his nose to the window of the plane and looked out at the ground below. This must be Morgan, he thought. It certainly didn't look anything like New York. For one thing, the buildings here were all short and wide, instead of tall and narrow the way they were at home. And everything was spread out; there was lots of space between one building and the next. Why, Fenton could even see grass around some of them!

"Well," said Fenton's father, leaning toward the window, "somewhere over there is the Sleeping Bear Mountain formation, with the dig site where I'll be working." He pointed toward a ridge of greenish-brown mountains in the distance.

"All the way over there?" asked Fenton, amazed. At home in New York, his father had only to walk across the street to go to work. "Why is it so far away from Morgan?"

"Oh, it's not far," said his father. "A couple of miles."

Fenton was confused. "But isn't *this* Morgan?" he asked, pointing out the window at the buildings below.

His father chuckled. "Oh, no," he said. "This is Cheyenne. Morgan's about sixty miles away. Someone from the dig site is supposed to pick us up at the airport and drive us there."

"Well, why didn't we just take a plane to Morgan, then?" asked Fenton.

"There is no airport in Morgan," said his father. "It's just a tiny little town. Why, we probably can't even see it from here."

Fenton pressed his nose against the foggy plastic window and didn't say anything. He stuck his hand into his jean-jacket pocket and felt something smooth and heavy—his mother's maiasaur paperweight. He had forgotten to give it back to her last night. Right now his mother was on a plane to India. Fenton tried not to think about the way he had felt saying good-bye to her in New York.

A few minutes later, Fenton and his father stood in the airport with their luggage. Fenton spotted a tall, heavy-set man in dusty jeans and a cowboy hat. In his hands was a ragged piece of cardboard with RUMPLEMAYER scrawled on it.

"Over there, Dad!" said Fenton.

The man's face broke into a grin as Fenton and his father headed over toward him.

"Hi, there!" he said, extending his hand to Fenton's father. "You must be Bill Rumplemayer. I'm Charlie Smalls."

"Ah, yes, Dr. Smalls, I'm familiar with your work," said Bill Rumplemayer, his hand pumping up and down in the other man's grip.

"Please, call me Charlie," said the man. "Everyone does."

"All right, Charlie," said Fenton's father. "This is my son, Fenton."

"Howdy do, Fenton," said Charlie, grinning hugely again, so that Fenton couldn't help but smile back.

Charlie picked up two of their three suitcases, tucked the third easily under one of his big arms, and headed out the door to a mud-and-dust-covered pickup truck with the round insignia of Wyoming State University on its door.

Charlie tossed the suitcases through the air and into the back of the pickup.

"You might enjoy the ride more back here," he said to Fenton. "It's kind of crowded with three up front. Besides, the view's better."

"Okay, Charlie, sure," said Fenton, scrambling over the side of the pickup. This was exciting. He'd never ridden in the back of a truck before.

The truck started with a lurch, and Fenton held on as it made its way out of the airport and onto a highway, eventually turning onto a smaller road with flat, dry, grassy plains on both sides. Fenton lay back in the truck against the suitcases. He had never seen so much sky. He gazed at the greenish-brown mountains in the distance and was amazed to see patches of white near their peaks. He squinted. Could that really be snow up there? How could there be snow in the summer?

After about an hour, the truck slowed down, and small

buildings began to appear on the side of the road. Fenton saw several houses and a small gas station go by. None of the buildings was more than two stories high. Then they passed something called the Morgan Market. This must be Morgan. It sure didn't look like much.

As the truck turned a corner onto a side street, Fenton noticed a weather-beaten hand-painted sign in front of a small, red building. WADSWORTH MUSEUM OF ROCKS & OTHER NATURAL CURIOS, it said. A rock museum—now that sounded kind of interesting. But what did "other natural curios" mean? The building behind the sign seemed way too small to be a museum; it was barely the size of a small house.

They turned onto an unpaved road, the truck bumping over dirt and rocks. Fenton clutched the side as the suitcases bounced around him. Was this still Morgan? There was nothing here but dry grass, a few bushes, and the mountains in the distance. Where was Charlie taking them?

Soon they passed a cluster of mailboxes stuck into the ground on sticks, and the truck made a sharp turn off the road. It bumped up a small rise and came to a stop. Fenton sat up straight and looked around. In front of the truck sat a two-story white house with a large porch on one side. Parked in the driveway was a second truck, just like the one they were in.

"Here we are," said Charlie, stepping out of the pickup. "Hope it didn't get too rough back there for you, Fenton."

Fenton looked at the house, amazed. Was this really where

MORGAN
MARKET

they were going to live? The house had a big red front door, green-shuttered windows, and a slanted shingled roof. It reminded Fenton of the kind of house he'd seen in storybooks for little kids, like something the Three Bears would live in. He certainly didn't know anyone who lived in a place like this.

He followed his father and Charlie inside. The house was cool and dark, and it took Fenton's eyes a moment to adjust.

"Yes, well, this will suit us just fine," Fenton's father said.

"The pickup in the driveway is yours," Charlie said, "but I thought you might need a hand getting started so I made a stop for you down at the Morgan Market this morning and picked up a few things—some fruit and cold cuts and stuff. It's all in the kitchen."

Fenton looked around. The room they were in must be the living room. It was bigger than their living room at home, and there was a fireplace in one wall. The movers had been there; the place was full of the boxes and furniture from New York. It seemed odd to see these familiar things here in this strange house. Especially since nothing was arranged the way it had been at home—the couch was facing a wall, and the shelves that had been in Fenton's bedroom were here in the living room.

Fenton wondered if his father would do something about the mess. He knew his mother would have gotten to work right away, organizing things. But Bill Rumplemayer hardly seemed to notice.

"So, Charlie," said his father, sitting down on one of the boxes, "why don't you fill me in on what the university team has been doing over at Sleeping Bear Mountain?"

"Sure thing, Bill," said Charlie.

Soon, Fenton's father and Charlie were deep in conversation. Fenton decided to explore the rest of the house.

The living room opened onto a large dining room. Fenton noticed his bedroom rug rolled up in a corner near the big flat box with his bicycle in it. It sure was going to be a huge job to get all this stuff into the right rooms of the house.

Next to the dining room was the kitchen. Everything there was yellow—the walls, the counters, even the stove and refrigerator. Fenton grabbed a bunch of grapes from a bowl of fruit on the counter and began popping them into his mouth.

He climbed the stairs at the end of the hall near the kitchen and found two large bedrooms and a bathroom on the second floor. He wondered which room was supposed to be his. It was impossible to tell because, as in the rest of the house, the furniture in these rooms was all jumbled together.

Then Fenton noticed a ladder leading up into the ceiling of one of the bedrooms. He climbed up and found himself in a large empty room with low, wooden ceilings that were slanted like the roof outside. This must be the attic.

There were several tiny windows in the slanted ceilings, and Fenton found that he could see in every direction around the house. A low wooden shelf ran around three of the room's four walls. Right away Fenton knew that he wanted the attic for his bedroom. Not only was it bigger than the two second-floor bedrooms, but the windows made it seem almost like a lookout tower. And the shelves would be perfect for his collection of dinosaur books.

He hurried back downstairs to the living room, where his father and Charlie were still talking.

"Hey, Dad, can I sleep in the attic?" asked Fenton.

The two men looked up.

"But aren't there two bedrooms?" asked his father, his forehead wrinkling a little. "They assured me at the museum that the house would have a bedroom for each of us."

"There are two," said Fenton. "But I like the attic better."

"Then I don't see why not," said Fenton's father. "I suppose I can use the second bedroom as my study."

"Hey, can we set up the computer soon, Dad?" asked Fenton, suddenly excited about contacting Max later that night. He sure had a lot to tell him about.

"Yes, in just a little while, son," answered his father. "Let me finish up here with Charlie."

Fenton noticed his skateboard sticking out of a crate near the coffee table.

"Maybe I'll go outside for a while," he said.

"There's a lot of land around here to explore, Fenton," said Charlie, smiling.

"Okay, see you later," Fenton sang out, grabbing his skateboard and banging through the side door.

But as he skipped down the porch steps, he realized something. There wasn't a smooth surface in sight anywhere. How was he supposed to skateboard when the ground was covered with grass, dirt, and rocks? He sighed, and sat down on the porch step. What kind of place was this where people couldn't even skateboard if they wanted to?

Fenton looked around. He could see the mountains in the distance, behind a clump of pine trees in the back of the house. A path led into the trees, and he decided to follow it. There had to be someplace he could skateboard around here.

As Fenton walked down the path, his board tucked under his arm, he saw a yellow house through the trees in the distance. He wondered how many blocks away it would be if it were in New York. It seemed like at least five, but it was hard to tell. Everything looked so different here.

Then the path turned a corner and came to a small clearing with a wooden shed at one end. The shed was small, about the size of the stand near the museum where his parents bought the newspaper every morning, and it looked pretty old. It was a pretty safe guess that no one lived there, thought Fenton, taking a couple of steps toward it.

Just then a twig cracked under Fenton's foot.

"Stop right there!" called a voice from inside the shack.

Fenton froze, startled.

"Who's there?" demanded the voice.

"Um, Fenton Rumplemayer," answered Fenton.

A boy's head poked out from the doorway.

"Who?" he asked again, screwing up his face.

"Uh, I'm Fenton," Fenton tried again.

"Hi," said the boy, stepping out into view. He was a few inches shorter than Fenton, with jet-black hair, blue jeans, and a green-and-white-striped T-shirt. "I'm Willy Whitefox."

"Do you live here?" asked Fenton.

"Nah, this is my clubhouse," answered Willy. "I live next door." He jerked his thumb at the yellow house in the distance.

"Oh. I live in the white house back there." It seemed odd to say it.

"Really?" said Willy, his face brightening. "Did you just move in or something?"

Fenton nodded.

"Is that yours?" Willy indicated the skateboard tucked under Fenton's arm.

Fenton nodded again, feeling his face grow hot. The idea of looking for a place to skateboard out here in the pine trees was starting to seem pretty silly.

"So, who else is in the club?" he asked, trying to sound casual. If there was a club here, it might be important to know about, but he didn't want to seem overeager, either.

Willy grinned. "Actually, no one," he admitted. "Just me, so far."

"Oh," said Fenton, a little surprised. He had never heard of a club with only one member.

"When I heard you outside, I thought you were my little sister," said Willy. "She's always trying to butt in on me. You want to come inside?"

"Okay," said Fenton, stepping forward.

The light in the shack was dim, and Willy turned on a flashlight. Fenton looked around. On the floor were a few wood crates and several large stacks of comic books.

Willy sat down on the floor, and Fenton did the same, putting his skateboard down beside him.

"You like comic books?" asked Willy.

Fenton shrugged. "They're okay."

"I probably have the biggest comic-book collection in Morgan," said Willy. "Where did you move here from?"

"The City," Fenton told him.

"Cheyenne?"

Fenton shook his head. Everyone he knew referred to New York as "the City." But Willy hadn't understood.

"New York City," Fenton explained.

Willy's eyes widened. "Wow; what's that like?"

"You've never been there?" asked Fenton.

Willy shook his head. "I've only been places in Wyoming."

"Oh," said Fenton. He couldn't imagine never having been away from where he lived. Fenton went to stay with his grandparents in Florida every year. And he had even been to California once to visit his cousins. "New York is a really cool place to live," he said. "My apartment—well, the one I used to live in—is right across the street from the New York Museum of Natural History. They have dinosaur fossils from all over the world there. And my friend Max—he lives in my building, too—he invented his own computer game called Treasure Quest. We used to play it practically every day."

"Do you have your own computer?" asked Willy.

"In New York I used Max's, but here we have one in the house. It's there because of my dad's work. He's in charge of this dig site where they're looking for dinosaurs."

"No kidding," said Willy. "Real dinosaurs, for real, here in Morgan?"

"I guess so," said Fenton. "I mean, they must dig up some of the bones around here. But then they send them all to the Museum of Natural History in New York. They have dinosaur bones from all over the world at the museum. I used to go there practically every day."

"Wow," said Willy. "You must know a lot about dinosaurs. Hey, what's the biggest dinosaur there is?"

"Well, that depends what you mean by the biggest," said Fenton. "The longest dinosaur is seismosaurus, which grew to over a hundred and forty feet. But ultrasaurus was heavier than seismosaurus—maybe a hundred tons or more."

"Cool," said Willy appreciatively. "What's the fastest?"

"Probably one of the ornithomimids," Fenton answered. They may have run at twenty-five miles per hour. They lived in the Cretaceous."

"Where's that?" asked Willy

"Not where, when. The Cretaceous is a period of time during the Mesozoic Era," explained Fenton. "The Mesozoic Era is when the dinosaurs lived. It's divided into three periods—the Triassic, the Jurassic, and the Cretaceous."

"So where's this place your father works?" asked Willy.

"Oh, near someplace called Sleeping Something-or-other," said Fenton, shrugging.

"Sleeping Bear Mountain," said Willy, nodding. "There's kind of a cool story about how that place got its name."

"Oh yeah?" said Fenton.

"Supposedly it's named after this bear that used to live there a long time ago," said Willy. "But they say one night he got frozen into solid rock by this icy cold stream."

"You're kidding," said Fenton. He had never heard anything like that before.

"Really," said Willy. "At least that's how the story goes. You can still see the rock if you go up near the top of the mountain."

"Where'd you hear this?" asked Fenton.

"My grandmother told me," explained Willy. "She's Arapaho."

"What's that?" asked Fenton.

"It's Native American," said Willy. "My whole family's Arapaho."

"Wow," said Fenton. He had never met anyone who was Native American before. He wasn't sure, but he didn't think there were too many Arapahos in New York.

"If you want, I can show you where Sleeping Bear Rock is sometime," said Willy. "Do you have a bike?"

Fenton nodded. He liked the idea of riding to Sleeping Bear Rock with Willy. In New York, he had only been able to ride his bike in Central Park, and then only if one of his parents went with him.

Suddenly Fenton thought of his father back at the house. He wondered how long he had been sitting here with Willy.

"I guess I'd better get going," he said. "My father and I have to unpack and stuff." He stood up from the crate, picked up his skateboard, and headed toward the door.

"Hey, Fenton," called Willy.

Fenton turned.

"I guess now that you live here, you're sort of in the club too," said Willy. "If you want to be, that is."

Fenton grinned. "Okay, Willy, thanks," he said, waving and running off toward the white house in the distance.

4

Fenton popped the last of his turkey sandwich into his mouth and anxiously checked the clock in the bright yellow kitchen stove again. Eight o'clock—exactly half an hour until it was time to contact Max. Luckily, his father had just finished setting up the computer in the study.

Fenton and his father had spent most of the evening moving boxes around and assembling furniture, and they were exhausted. Charlie had helped with the heavier pieces before he left, so at least now everything was in the right room. But there were still a lot of boxes to unpack. And since Fenton's mother had been the one to fill most of the boxes back in New York, Fenton and his father were having a hard time finding things now without her.

"I have an idea," said Fenton's father, after emptying the fourth box in a row looking for their pajamas. "Let's give your mother a quick call and say hello."

"In India?" said Fenton excitedly. He had never talked to anyone as far away as that before.

"Sure," said Mr. Rumplemayer. He looked at his watch. "She should be settled into her hotel in Delhi by now."

Fenton's father picked up the phone and punched in what seemed to Fenton like way too many numbers for just one phone call. He got through to the hotel, and handed the phone to Fenton, who waited while the clerk rang his mother's room.

When she answered, her voice sounded very far away.

"Hello?"

"Hi, Mom."

"Hi, honey!" said Fenton's mother, her voice growing louder. "I was hoping it would be you! How are you? How's the house? Are you and Dad settling in all right?"

Fenton told her all about his attic bedroom and Willy and the shack and how Sleeping Bear Mountain got its name. He didn't tell her about the ride in the back of the pickup truck, though. Somehow he didn't think she would like the idea too much. He did tell her that he and his father had been looking for their pajamas.

"The labels on the boxes are all color coded," she explained. "I told all this to your father in New York, but I suppose he forgot. All the boxes with summer clothes in them are labeled with your names in green marker, and the clothes I thought you would need right away, like pajamas, have a green star on the box too."

"Okay," said Fenton. It felt good to have his mother taking care of things again. "What's India like?" he asked. "Have you seen any tigers?"

His mother laughed. "Not yet," she said. "Mostly just lots of people and cars. But that's because I'm in the city now. In a few days I'll be getting on a train to Kapoor, the first village I'll be staying at. First I have to try to get some rest, though. I'm tired after that long plane ride. But it's almost seven-thirty in the morning here now, the beginning of a new day."

"Seven-thirty in the morning!" repeated Fenton.

"That's right," said his mother. "There's a big time difference between the United States and India, you know—I'll be eating my breakfast in a few minutes."

Oh, right, time zones, thought Fenton. He knew that the time of day was always different in different parts of the world, but somehow it still seemed impossible that his mother could be getting ready to eat breakfast when he and his father would be going to bed soon.

"Okay, honey, let me talk to Dad for a few minutes," his mother said. "I'll try to give you a call or write you soon."

As Fenton said good-bye to his mother and handed the phone to his father, he suddenly had a thought—there was a time difference between New York and other parts of the United States, wasn't there? He looked at the kitchen clock and tried to think as he waited for his father to get off the telephone. Eight-twenty—ten minutes until he was supposed to contact Max. But was it eight-twenty where Max was?

"Dad, what time is it in New York right now?" he asked as soon as his father hung up the phone.

"New York? Well, they're two hours ahead of us, so that would make it—almost ten-thirty P.M."

Ten-thirty! That meant Fenton was two hours late for Max! He hurried up to the second floor, turned on the computer, activated the modem, and punched in Max's number.

]HI MAX. ITS FENTON[

he typed.

He waited, but there was no answer. Max must have turned off his computer and gone to bed.

Suddenly that was just where Fenton wanted to be—in bed. He decided to find the box labeled in green with his name and the star. He'd try to reach Max again tomorrow night.

Ten minutes later, after saying good night to his father, Fenton lay in his sleeping bag on his bed in the attic. But somehow, even though he was in his familiar bed, he didn't feel right. Just a few minutes ago he had been so sleepy; now his eyes wouldn't stay closed.

It was awfully quiet here. There weren't any traffic sounds outside. And the moonlight that streamed in through the windows in the slanted ceiling was nothing like the light from the street that had lit up his old room every night.

Fenton sat up in bed. In the moonlight he could see the

boxes his mother had packed stacked around the attic. His jean jacket lay across one of them. He slipped out of bed and reached into the pocket.

With the heavy glass object in his hand, he made his way back across the room. He placed the maiasaur paperweight on the low shelf directly under one of the windows, where he could see it clearly in the moonlight.

He climbed back under the covers, his eyes on the tiny dinosaur curled up inside its egg. It was the last thing he saw as he drifted off to sleep.

"Fenton! Fenton!"

Fenton opened his eyes, trying to figure out where he was. Then he remembered—his new room in Morgan, Wyoming. He hopped out of bed and hurried over to the window above the shelf where he had put the maiasaur paperweight the night before. Standing in back of the house was Willy, a red bicycle lying on the grass beside him.

"Fenton!" yelled Willy again, cupping his hands to his mouth.

Fenton struggled to open the little window. "Willy! Hi! Up here!"

"Hi!" said Willy, looking up and shading his eyes. "Do you want to ride over to Sleeping Bear with me?"

"Okay," said Fenton. "Hang on, I'll be right there."

He opened one of the boxes with the green labels and

yanked out the first clothes he could find—a pair of shorts and his New York Mets T-shirt. As he pulled the T-shirt over his head, he wondered if Willy liked the Mets. Probably he rooted for another team. Fenton knew there was no Wyoming team, but he couldn't remember what teams were near Wyoming either. Maybe the Colorado Rockies.

In the kitchen, Fenton found a note from his father.

Fenton—I have gone to the dig site.
See you later. Have fun exploring.
—Dad

He grabbed an apple from the fruit bowl on the counter and headed out the side door.

"Hey, nice bike," said Willy as Fenton wheeled his shiny blue ten-speed out of the garage.

"Thanks," said Fenton proudly.

"Those tires are kind of thin, though," said Willy. "Maybe you could get some mountain-bike tires put on your bike, like I have. They're better on rough roads and grass and stuff."

Fenton looked at the fat tires on Willy's bike and shrugged.

"Mine'll probably be all right," he said.

"Okay," said Willy, straddling his bike, "but if you change your mind, I can show you where the bike store is in town."

Fenton tossed his apple core into a bush, and the two boys set off down the dirt road, Willy in the lead. When they got to the end, they made a right on the paved road, away from Morgan and toward the mountain.

Fenton pedaled alongside Willy, his bicycle bumping over the cracks in the road. A split-rail fence ran along a field to their left, and Fenton could see horses in the distance.

"That's the Carr Ranch," said Willy.

"What's a car ranch?" asked Fenton.

"Not a car ranch, the Carr Ranch, C-A-R-R," said Willy. "It's a horse ranch. The Carr family owns it."

Fenton stared, amazed. The fence seemed to go on forever. Did one family really own all that land?

The road grew narrower as it approached the mountains. The sun was getting stronger, and Fenton was beginning to feel hot. He wondered how far they had gone. He was pretty sure he had never ridden this far on his bike before.

Then Willy turned off the paved road and onto a dirt one. Fenton's tires skidded as he pedaled after him, his bike unsteady on the rocky road. Meanwhile, Willy's bike crunched easily over the gravel and dirt. Fenton pedaled furiously, hoping he wouldn't puncture a tire on the rocks. Maybe he should take Willy's advice about getting thicker tires after all.

They began to climb uphill, and Fenton struggled to keep up. He switched to a lower gear, sweat pouring down his face. The sun beat down, and dust flew from under his tires. Just as Fenton was beginning to feel like he couldn't go on any longer, Willy pulled over to the side of the road.

"Okay, this is it." Willy leaned his bike against some scrubby bushes.

Fenton looked around, gasping a little for air. They were about halfway up the mountain, and the town of Morgan lay spread out below them. Fenton could even make out his house and Willy's nestled into one of the lower ridges.

"Wow," he said. "This is almost like being in an airplane."

Willy grinned.

"So where's this Sleeping Bear?" asked Fenton.

"Actually, it's all the way at the top," said Willy. "But you can see it pretty well from here." He pointed toward the mountain's peak.

"I don't see anything," said Fenton, shading his eyes.

"Try again," said Willy. "See that big rock?"

Fenton looked up. Suddenly he saw it—a huge piece of black rock, jutting out near the top of the mountain. It was exactly the shape of an enormous bear curled up on its side.

"Wow," said Fenton. "I can even see its ears!"

"Yeah, isn't it cool?" said Willy. "You know, they say that when the weather gets really hot like this, and the bear warms up, he thaws a little and comes back to life. My grandmother says that sometimes on a warm summer night you can hear the bear moaning and growling up here."

Just then Fenton heard a low growling sound in the distance, and jumped in spite of himself.

"What's that?" he asked Willy.

The two boys looked at each other, and suddenly Willy burst out laughing.

"Look!" he said, pointing back down the road.

Fenton turned. A pickup truck was approaching, its engine groaning with the effort of climbing the mountain road. As it got closer, he could see the university insignia on the door. Then he recognized the driver.

"Charlie!" called Fenton, waving.

The truck pulled to a stop at the side of the road, and Fenton and Willy ran over to it.

"Hi, Fenton," said Charlie, grinning.

"Hi, Charlie. This is my friend Willy."

Charlie tipped his hat. Fenton noticed that little rivers of sweat were rolling down his face. "Howdy do, Willy."

"Hi," said Willy.

"You boys ride all the way up here in this heat?" asked Charlie, wiping at his forehead with a bandanna. "Throw your bikes in the back, and I'll give you a ride the rest of the way."

"The rest of the way?" echoed Fenton. "Oh, you mean to the dig site?"

"Where the dinosaurs are?" asked Willy excitedly.

Charlie laughed. "Well," he said, "there aren't too many dinosaurs up there at the moment, although we sure are looking hard. We did uncover an interesting dinosaur footprint, though."

"Okay," said Fenton. After all, his father would be at the dig site, and Fenton was sure that he wouldn't mind if Fenton came by for a visit. Besides, the dig site was beginning to sound a little more interesting to him. He wouldn't mind taking a look at this footprint they had found. Up until now the only dinosaur tracks Fenton had ever seen up close were in a slab of rock that was mounted on a wall in the museum. Here was a chance to see a footprint in the actual ground where the dinosaur itself had walked.

Charlie helped them get their bikes into the back of the truck and opened the passenger door for them to climb in. As the motor started, Fenton was secretly a little disappointed not to be riding in the back, but judging by the way the bikes had begun to bounce around back there, he realized it probably was better to be up front, after all.

Charlie drove the truck about three miles farther up the mountain, then pulled off on a level dirt road. The road snaked between two peaks of the mountain, one of them with Sleeping Bear Rock at the top. In the distance Fenton could see the camp. There were a couple of long trailers, some makeshift tents, and a few more pickup trucks.

Charlie parked his truck, and they hopped out.

"So where are all the dinosaurs?" Willy asked Fenton under his breath.

Fenton looked around and shrugged. After all, he had never been to a dig site before either. So far it didn't look like anything special, just like any other spot in the area. He had the feeling that this wasn't going to be at all like finding his way around the museum in New York, where everything was assembled in displays and carefully labeled.

They followed Charlie to where Bill Rumplemayer was stooped over a patch of reddish dirt. Squatting next to him was a woman in a big straw hat.

"Hey, Bill," Charlie called out as they got closer. "I brought you a little surprise." He indicated Fenton and Willy. "I found them riding their bikes up the mountain."

"Hi, Dad," said Fenton. "This is my friend Willy from next door."

"Why, hello, son," said Fenton's father. "Hello, Willy, it's nice to meet you. Boys, this is Professor Lily Martin, of the university." He indicated the woman in the hat. "Professor Martin, my son Fenton and our neighbor Willy."

Professor Martin looked up and smiled, her eyes squinting in the sunlight. Next to her on the ground was a red plastic tool kit, and in her hand was a blue toothbrush. The toothbrush seemed strange to Fenton. He wondered if Professor Martin had been brushing her teeth out at the site.

"Hello, boys," she said. "You're just in time to get a glimpse of our new discovery. Did Charlie tell you about it?"

"He said there was a dinosaur footprint," said Fenton. He looked around excitedly. "Where is it?"

Charlie laughed. "Why, you're practically standing on it."

Fenton looked down at the ground. All he could see were

rocks and dust. Then, suddenly, he spotted something—a raised mound of hard, reddish rock, a few inches high and about two feet long, with four toe-shaped points at one end. He hadn't noticed it at first because he had been looking for a footprint pressed *into* the ground. This shape rose up out of the ground.

He squatted down over the mound excitedly.

"Wow!" he said. "What dinosaur is it from, Dad?"

"We're not sure yet," said his father. "But we do know that the rock it's in is about a hundred million to a hundred and twenty million years old."

"So it's an Early-Cretaceous dinosaur," said Fenton.

Looking around, he began to imagine the area as it must have looked a hundred million years ago. The earth's climate was different back then; the landscape would have been filled with lush green tropical plants and some of the first flowers. If the dinosaur left its footprints in the mud, there must have been some water nearby, probably a large lake or inland sea.

Fenton's imagination filled in the scene with dinosaurs of the Cretaceous. He saw a group of nodosauruses, thickly set dinosaurs that walked on four feet and were protected by coats of heavy armor, stop to drink from the lake. Nearby, a medium-sized, strongly built tenontosaurus nibbled at a bush, its thick, massive tail twitching with pleasure.

Suddenly a pack of deinonychus dinosaurs on the hunt for food appeared, their eyes darting hungrily. The name deinonychus means "terrible claw," and these dinosaurs had sharp, curved, daggerlike claws on the second toes of their back feet. When the pack appeared, there was the pounding of feet as the herd of nodosauruses stampeded in fear. But they had nothing to worry about. The deinonychus pack passed right by the nodosauruses, sensing that the thick armor of a nodosaurus would be harder to get their claws through than the soft flesh of a tenontosaurus.

As the deinonychus pack approached, the tenontosaurus reared up on its hind legs, preparing to flee, but the deinonychuses were too fast for it. Leaping on their prey and holding tight with their strong front limbs, they kicked furiously at the tenontosaurus, using their sharp, knifelike toe claws as attack weapons. The tenontosaurus swung its massive tail, trying in vain to knock the savage pack off its body.

"Wow," said Willy, cutting into Fenton's thoughts. "A hundred million years ago—that's old!"

Fenton shook his head. The dinosaurs of the Cretaceous had vanished, and he was standing in the dry, sunny clearing again with the others.

"What else have you figured out about the dinosaur that made this print, Dad?" he asked, eager to know exactly what kind of dinosaur had left the footprint.

"Unfortunately, not too much," said Bill Rumplemayer. "What we really need now is to find some other prints. They'll help us determine the length of the dinosaur's stride and whether it was bipedal or quadrupedal."

"What does all that mean?" asked Willy.

"Bipedal means it walked on two feet, and quadrupedal means it walked on four feet," explained Fenton. "And stride means how far apart the steps were that the dinosaur took."

"That's right," said Charlie. "In general, the bigger the dinosaur, and the faster it was moving, the bigger the stride."

"There's one thing I don't understand, though," said Fenton. "Why is the shape of the dinosaur's foot sticking up out of the ground like that? If it's a footprint, shouldn't it be pressed *into* the ground instead?"

"It was pressed into the ground like a regular footprint when the dinosaur first made it," explained Mr. Rumplemayer. "But there must have been some shifting within the earth that turned it upside down."

Fenton nodded. He knew that over millions of years, forces under the ground had continually caused the land on the surface to shift, and that this shifting sometimes made bumps or wrinkles in the earth's surface. When the bumps were really big, they ended up as mountains, like the ones he could see in the distance. When they were smaller, they became hills and inclines.

"I don't get it," said Willy. "How can the ground be upside down?"

"Well," said Fenton, "shifting under the earth's surface makes parts of it move around. It's sort of like the way that moving your feet around under the covers in bed makes bumps and wrinkles in the blanket. Sometimes a layer of rock only gets moved to a new angle. But this rock must have kept being pushed around by the earth's shifting until it was completely upside down."

"Oh," said Willy, "so we're looking at the *other* side of the footprint, the underneath part."

"Exactly," said Charlie.

"That was an excellent explanation, Fenton," said Lily Martin, smiling. "You know, I could use your help explaining that idea to my college classes sometime."

Fenton grinned.

"What Professor Martin and I are trying to do now is to completely uncover these tracks," Fenton's father went on. "You see, when the dinosaur walked here, this rock was probably soft mud. As time went by, the mud got baked dry, hardened into rock, and was covered by new layers of dirt and soil. Older land surfaces are continually being covered up by newer ones, so if there are fossils of any kind hidden in them, they stay hidden until wind or rain exposes them a bit."

"That's right," said Lily Martin. "In fact, a couple of hours ago, most of this footprint was covered with rock, soil, and dirt. The only part that was visible was one of the toes."

She brushed carefully at the edge of the raised footprint with her toothbrush, clearing away some dirt.

"Oh," said Fenton, "so that's what that's for."

"Uncovering any fossil is a long and painstaking process," explained Fenton's father. "If you're not careful, you can destroy the thing you are trying to uncover. Toothbrushes and other dental tools are great for this sort of work."

That made a lot more sense to Fenton than the idea that Professor Martin had been brushing her teeth out here.

"But why do you keep calling the footprint a fossil?" asked Willy. "I thought fossils were bones."

"A fossil can be just about anything," explained Charlie. "Fossils that are bones or teeth or eggs are called body fossils. Footprints, claw marks, and anything else a dinosaur leaves behind are called trace fossils."

"So now our job is to uncover the rest of these particular trace fossils," said Lily Martin.

"The rest of them?" asked Willy excitedly. "Do you really think there are more?"

Charlie laughed. "Well, I don't know about you, but I've never known an animal to leave only one footprint," he said. "However, until we get some more information, exactly who made this footprint is going to remain something of a mystery."

Fenton felt himself shiver with excitement despite the hot sun on his back. This was great. At the museum, all the answers had been spelled out for him, all the dinosaur names listed on plaques. But this was a real dinosaur mystery, and suddenly Fenton couldn't think of anything more exciting!

5

Fenton tugged at the stack of boxes again, but it was no use—it wouldn't budge. He could see the box he was trying to get, the one labeled FENTON—DINO BOOKS. It was wedged into a corner of his room, with two other boxes on top of it and a stack of three boxes in front of it.

Sitting down on the edge of his bed, he took a bite of the turkey sandwich he had made and tried to think. He knew he could wait and ask his father help him move the boxes, but it was still afternoon, and his father wouldn't be home for hours. He really wanted to start looking up information on Cretaceous dinosaurs in his books right away. It had been that thought that had made him manage to pedal even faster than Willy on the bike ride home from the dig site. That, and the fact that most of the ride had been downhill, which hadn't been as hard to manage with his thin tires.

Then Fenton had an idea. The boxes wouldn't be nearly as heavy if he emptied them. He pulled over his desk chair and climbed onto it, ripping open the top box. The box was labeled with his name in green, and just as his mother had said, it was full of his summer clothes. Fenton grabbed a handful of folded T-shirts out of the top of the box and tossed them to the floor.

The box was still too heavy to lift. Fenton scooped out more clothes, dropping them onto the floor. Finally, when the box was a little more than half emptied, it was light enough for Fenton to move. Clutching it in his arms and climbing carefully down from the chair, he carried it to the other side of the room.

The next box was labeled in red and was filled with sheets and blankets for his bed. So that's where his dinosaur-print sheets were! He'd had them since he was a little kid, and they were still his favorites. He tossed them on his bed; maybe his father would put them on later. Soon that box was light enough to move too.

An hour later he had managed to move all the boxes that he needed to get to the one with the dinosaur books in it. His room was a wreck—there were sheets, blankets, games, and clothes for all seasons strewn everywhere. Even his favorite birthday present from last year—the tyrannosaurus-shaped alarm clock that roared when the alarm went off—was under a heap of clothes on the floor. But Fenton was too excited to care. As fast as he could, he tore open the top of the box, pulled out his thickest dinosaur encyclopedia, and sat down on the floor to start reading.

The hours passed by quickly as Fenton became absorbed in gathering information on Cretaceous dinosaurs. There were a lot of dinosaurs to look up, and he hadn't exactly found the answer yet, but there was no doubt in Fenton's mind that he was going to be able to solve the mystery.

Then, suddenly, in the middle of reading about craterosaurus, an Early-Cretaceous dinosaur from the stegosaurid family of dinosaurs, he slammed his book shut.

"Max!" he said out loud, remembering.

What time was it? Jumping up, he began rummaging through the piles of things on the floor, looking for his T-rex alarm clock.

When he finally managed to find it, he saw that the hands weren't even moving. It hadn't been wound since New York. The time said ten minutes after eleven.

"Awww!" he yelled, tossing the clock back onto the pile and hurrying toward the opening in the attic floor that led to the ladder.

In no time at all he was down the attic steps, through his father's study, and down the main stairs to the first floor of the house. He ran through the hall and into the kitchen, his socks sliding on the yellow linoleum floor.

The clock in the stove said six twenty-nine. That meant it was eight twenty-nine in New York. One minute to go. Fenton hurried back out the door and up the steps to the study. Turning on the computer, he activated the modem and keyed in Max's number. Hopefully Max had realized that something had happened last night and would be waiting again tonight.

]HI MAX. ITS ME. R U THERE? [

he typed, and waited.
Then came the response:

<**WHERE WERE U LAST NITE?**>

Max was there! It had worked!

]SORRY I FORGOT THE TIME ISNT THE SAME IN NY. THEN IT WAS 2 LATE + U WERE GONE[

Fenton keyed in happily.

<**OK**>

was Max's next response.

]HOW R U?[

<**GOOD I GUESS. WHATS IT LIKE THERE?**>

]DIFFERENT. LOTS OF LAND + HARDLY ANY BUILDINGS. WE LIVE IN A REAL HOUSE. MY ROOM IS THE ATTIC[

<**COOL**>

]BUT THERES NOWHERE 2 SKATEBOARD. HOWS NY?[

<**SAME AS USUAL. ITS HOT OUT. GUS IS QUITTING**>

]GUS THE DOORMAN?[

<RIGHT. HES RETIRING. THE BUILDINGS GIVING HIM A PARTY IN THE LOBBY THE DAY AFTER TOMORROW. I GUESS U R GOING 2 MISS IT>

]I GUESS SO. I MET A KID NAMED WILLY. HE LIVES NEXT DOOR. TODAY WE WENT TO THE DIG SITE. THERE WAS A DINO FOOTPRINT. WE DONT KNOW WHAT KIND YET[

<SOUNDS FUN. WANT TO PLAY TQ NOW?>

]OK[

At first it felt funny to play Treasure Quest without actually sitting next to Max in his room. Soon Fenton was involved in the game, though, and he almost forgot where he was.

Toward the end of the third game, Fenton heard his father come into the house and realized that he was hungry. It must be time for dinner by now. When the game was over, he signed off, promising to contact Max at the same time the next night.

"Hi, Dad!" he called, bounding down the stairs and into the kitchen.

But his father wasn't in the kitchen.

"Dad?" called Fenton again.

"In here," came the reply from the living room.

Fenton found his father sitting on the couch.

"What are you doing?" asked Fenton.

"Oh, just trying to rest a little," sighed Mr. Rumplemayer.

"Working at the dig site sure takes a lot more out of me than being in the lab ever did. I'm not used to spending so much time on my feet—or my knees, for that matter. And that hot sun doesn't make it any easier."

Fenton noticed that his father's face was bright red. It looked like he had a sunburn.

"Gee, Dad, maybe you should wear a hat or something," he said, thinking of the big straw hat Lily Martin had worn.

"You're probably right, son," said his father, raising his hand to touch his nose. "Ouch. I'm afraid I may be too late."

Fenton felt his stomach growl. "Hey, Dad, what's for dinner?" he asked.

"Dinner, that's right!" said Mr. Rumplemayer. "I suppose we should see what's in the fridge."

"Okay," said Fenton, following his father into the kitchen.

"Hmmm," said Mr. Rumplemayer, peering into the refrigerator. "Well, we still have some of those cold cuts that Charlie got. There's turkey and roast beef."

"I'll have roast beef," said Fenton. After having eaten turkey sandwiches for lunch and for dinner the night before, he was kind of sick of them. In fact, he was starting to feel a little tired of sandwiches in general.

"Well, Fenton," said his father a moment later, handing Fenton his sandwich, "I have some news from the dig site that might interest you."

"What is it?" asked Fenton, biting into his roast beef. "Did you find another footprint?"

"We sure did," said Bill Rumplemayer, smiling. "Another four-toed print. The dinosaur's other hind foot, it looks like."

"That's great, Dad!" said Fenton, chewing. "That means that now you can measure the stride length, which will help you decide how long the dinosaur was, right?"

"Exactly," said his father, taking a bite of his own sandwich. "I plan to get started on the calculations to figure it out tomorrow."

"Hey, can Willy and I come out and look at the new print tomorrow?" asked Fenton excitedly.

"Sure, Fenton, any time you want to ride your bike out to the dig site when I'm there is fine," answered Mr. Rumplemayer.

Fenton thought of something. "Can I go into town and get some new tires for my bike first?" he asked. "Mine are kind of hard to ride with around here, and Willy said he'd show me where there's a bike store where I can get mountain-bike tires like his."

"That sounds like a good idea," agreed his father. "Sturdier tires will probably be safer on these roads."

Fenton gulped down the rest of his food. Another footprint at the site, and new tires for his bike! He could hardly wait for tomorrow.

6

"Hey, Willy, what's that place up ahead?" asked Fenton as the two of them rode into town on their bikes the next day. He pointed to the small red building that he had first noticed on the drive from the airport, the one with the sign that said WADSWORTH MUSEUM OF ROCKS & OTHER NATURAL CURIOS. "Is it really a museum?"

"Sure," said Willy, pedaling alongside him. "Old Mrs. Wadsworth runs it. She's really nice. Maybe we can go in there and see her later on, after we drop your bike off at the shop."

"Okay," said Fenton, shrugging. The small red building still looked more like a house than a museum to him, but he was curious to see it inside.

They cut across the museum's dirt parking lot and past a small flower garden. A sprinkler watering the garden was also watering the parking lot and had made a muddy puddle. As the boys' bikes splashed through the puddle, Fenton noticed the wide track left by Willy's thick tires in the mud. He looked over his shoulder to see his own tire track. Right now his bike left only a skinny trail, but soon he would have thick tires like

Willy's. Excited, Fenton pumped harder at his pedals. He couldn't wait to get his new tires and to try them out on the road to the dig site this afternoon.

When they arrived at the bike shop, Willy jumped off his bike and leaned it against a tree near the road.

"Come on, Fenton," he said. "Let's bring your bike inside."

"But what about *your* bike?" asked Fenton. "You're not going to just leave it out here, are you?"

"Sure," said Willy. "No need to bring mine in too."

"But won't someone steal it?" asked Fenton. "I mean, shouldn't you lock it up or something?"

"Steal it? In the middle of the *day?*" said Willy, screwing up his face in disbelief. "No way, it's fine here."

Fenton was amazed. In New York, no one would ever leave a bicycle outside for even a minute without locking it up first. But he supposed things were different here in Morgan.

Inside, Fenton and Willy explained what they wanted to the man behind the counter, who told them to come back for Fenton's bicycle in a couple of hours.

Sure enough, when they came out, Willy's bike was still leaning against the tree out front. It hadn't been stolen.

"Let's go see Mrs. Wadsworth at the museum while we're waiting," suggested Willy. "I'll ride you there on my bike."

Fenton climbed onto the seat of Willy's bike, and Willy stepped onto the pedals, straddling the bar in front. They had a little trouble getting started, but soon they were riding back toward the Wadsworth Museum, Fenton balancing on the seat, and Willy standing up in front of him, pumping the pedals.

A few minutes later they rode across the museum's dirt parking lot, through the mud puddle by the garden, and toward the small red building. Willy leaned his bike against the wooden sign out front, and the two boys headed up the steps. The bells on the door jangled as Willy pushed it open.

"Just a minute!" called out a woman's voice from the back.

Fenton looked around. They were standing in a small room that was filled with shelves, tables, display stands, and counters of all sizes, all pushed up against each other. In some places the furniture was crammed so closely together that there was hardly any room to stand. *What kind of museum is this?* he wondered. *There's barely even enough room for visitors.*

Then he began to notice some of the objects that were crowded onto the shelves and the tops of the tables and counters. There were rocks of all different sizes, which didn't really surprise him—after all, this was supposed to be a rock museum. In front of each rock was a tiny, hand-lettered sign telling its name: SANDSTONE, LIMESTONE, GRANITE.

But in addition to the rocks, there was an amazing variety of other objects on display. Fenton saw several birds' nests, some butterflies pinned to a board, and even a necklace made out of some kind of animal teeth. *These must be the "Other Natural Curios" advertised on the sign outside,* he thought, looking around in amazement. He had definitely never seen a museum like this before.

Just then a woman came through a door in the back of the room. Her thin white hair was swept into a bun on top of her head, and a pair of glasses shaped like half-moons sat on the tip of her nose. She looked like a storybook grandmother. But she sure wasn't dressed like one. This woman wore an old, mud-stained white T-shirt and baggy blue overalls. On her feet was a pair of sturdy brown hiking boots.

"Why, Willy Whitefox!" she said, breaking into a huge smile. "You've come to visit and brought a friend! How marvelous!"

"Hi, Mrs. Wadsworth," said Willy. "This is Fenton Rumplemayer. He just moved to Morgan."

"I'm very pleased to make your acquaintance, Fenton," said Mrs. Wadsworth. "You boys are just in time to see my latest find. It's in the back. Why don't you come and have some lunch."

Fenton was glad Mrs. Wadsworth had mentioned lunch. He was starting to get hungry. He and Willy followed Mrs. Wadsworth through the maze of counters and tables, and into a second, smaller room. In the center of the room was a table and four chairs. Against one wall was a bed, and across the room from that were an old sink, refrigerator, and stove. Something was bubbling in a pot on top of the stove.

"Welcome to my little home," said Mrs. Wadsworth, picking up a big spoon and walking toward the stove.

Fenton looked around. The place was pretty small, but there was something about it he liked. It must be fun to live here, with all those rocks and things right in the next room.

Mrs. Wadsworth began to stir the pot on the stove, and Fenton and Willy pulled out chairs and sat down at the table. Fenton wondered what they were having for lunch. It must be some kind of soup, he thought. Or maybe even spaghetti.

But then Mrs. Wadsworth reached into the pot and pulled out one of the strangest-looking things Fenton had ever seen. Suddenly he realized what it was—the skull of an animal, with two large, branch-shaped horns sticking out of the top of it. Fenton stared.

"What do you think, boys?" asked Mrs. Wadsworth, gazing down at the skull.

Fenton didn't know what to say. He hoped this didn't have anything to do with lunch.

"It's an elk, right?" said Willy excitedly.

"That's right," said Mrs. Wadsworth happily. "I found it a couple of miles out on the road to Cheyenne. I figure it must have been killed by a cougar or something." She looked down at the skull and smiled. "It's just lovely, isn't it?"

Fenton gulped. He looked at Willy, who was still grinning at the elk skull. Fenton was definitely starting to get worried—

what if elk-head soup turned out to be some kind of Wyoming specialty or something?

"I'd say a few more minutes in boiling water and it should be completely clean," said Mrs. Wadsworth, dropping the skull back into the pot. "And I know just the perfect spot for it in the museum. Now, how about some hot dogs for you boys?"

"Hot dogs, great!" Fenton blurted out, in relief. The elk head didn't have anything to do with lunch after all.

A few minutes later Mrs. Wadsworth put three hot dogs and three mugs of cold lemonade on the table and pulled out a chair for herself. "Now, Fenton, tell me, where have you come from, and what brings you to Morgan?"

"Well," said Fenton, taking a bite of his hot dog, "I'm from the Cit—" He stopped. He didn't want to make that mistake again. "I'm from New York City."

"Fenton's father is looking for dinosaurs at Sleeping Bear," added Willy.

"Dinosaurs, how marvelous!" said Mrs. Wadsworth. "And is your father finding many dinosaurs, Fenton?"

"Well, so far he and his team have found some tracks," said Fenton. "But they're not sure just what kind of dinosaur they're from."

"They just found a new footprint yesterday afternoon," said Willy excitedly. "We're going out there today to see it."

"My goodness, how terribly thrilling," said Mrs. Wadsworth, chewing on her hot dog, her cheeks flushed pink.

"There's nothing quite like discovering something out in the field. In fact, Sleeping Bear has always been one of my favorite places to hunt for specimens. Not that I've ever found a dinosaur, mind you, but I have collected some very interesting rocks. And I got some lovely feathers from an old eagle's nest out there."

"Well, if you found feathers, that's kind of like finding a dinosaur, Mrs. Wadsworth," said Fenton. "You see, a lot of scientists believe some later types of dinosaurs grew feathers and maybe even flew, which means that today's birds are probably descended from dinosaurs."

"Well, isn't that fascinating!" said Mrs. Wadsworth. "You certainly seem to have a lot of knowledge about dinosaurs, Fenton."

"Fenton knows everything there is to know about dinosaurs," said Willy proudly.

Fenton felt his face flush. "Well, maybe not everything," he said. "For instance, I still don't know what kind of dinosaur made those tracks up at Sleeping Bear." He took a deep breath. "But I do plan to find out."

"Good for you, Fenton," said Mrs. Wadsworth, peering at him over her half-moon spectacles as she refilled his mug. "With that kind of determination, I believe you will find out."

"We should probably go now, Mrs. Wadsworth," said Willy. "We have to pick up Fenton's bike at the shop."

"I'll walk outside with you," said Mrs. Wadsworth, standing up. She reached into the pot and pulled out the elk skull. "I want to let this sit in the sun for a while to dry out."

"Thanks for lunch, Mrs. Wadsworth," said Fenton as the three of them made their way back through the front room and outside.

"My pleasure, boys. You come back anytime." She placed her free hand over her eyes to shield them from the sun. "Oh, I suppose those flowers have had enough water for now. And look at that big puddle. Willy, do me a favor, please, and run around back and turn off that sprinkler."

"Sure, Mrs. Wadsworth," said Willy, jogging around the side of the building.

"Good-bye, Fenton," said Mrs. Wadsworth, placing the elk skull down on the top step. "Come back and visit again soon."

"Good-bye, Mrs. Wadsworth, thanks," said Fenton.

As Mrs. Wadsworth headed back inside, Fenton glanced at the mud puddle in the parking lot, still streaked with tire tracks from the bicycles. Suddenly he noticed something interesting. In addition to the skinny trail that his own bike had made the first time they rode by the museum, there appeared to be two types of thicker trails. One of them had a simple V-shaped pattern. The other tire track had the same V-shaped pattern in the center, but with a dotted-line pattern on either side. Well, thought Fenton, I guess someone else with slightly different mountain-bike tires rode through here too.

Wondering which of the tracks had been left by Willy, he

bent down to look at the tires of Willy's bike. In addition to the raised, V-shaped pattern in the center, he saw two ridges of rubber that looked like broken lines on the outermost edges of each tire.

"What are you doing, Fenton?" asked Willy, wiping his hands on his jeans as he came back around the corner.

"Nothing, really," Fenton answered. "Just trying to figure out which tire tracks are from your bike." He indicated the two thick sets of tracks in the mud.

"That's easy," said Willy, pointing to the simpler pattern, the one without the broken lines. "This one's mine."

"No way," said Fenton, pointing to the rubber ridge of broken lines on the outermost edges of Willy's bike tires. "See, it has to be the other track."

"Fenton," said Willy, "I've been riding this bike in the dirt for two years. I know what my own tire tracks look like."

"Let's try it," suggested Fenton. "Ride your bike through the puddle again and we'll look. It'll be like an experiment."

"Okay," said Willy, "but you'll see."

Fenton watched as Willy mounted his bike and rode it through the puddle and back again.

"What did I tell you?" said Willy, pointing triumphantly at the fresh tracks he had made.

Fenton looked down at the mud in astonishment. As Willy had predicted, the new tire tracks showed only the V-shaped pattern, and nothing of the dotted-line pattern from the edges.

"Those other tracks must be from someone else," said Willy.

"I guess so," said Fenton, still finding it hard to believe. He had been so certain that the other tracks had been made by Willy's bike. But apparently the dotted lines on the outer edges of Willy's tires didn't even touch the ground when he rode.

"Come on," said Willy. "Let's get back to the bike store. After all, it's *your* bike tires we should be looking at."

"Oh, right," said Fenton, remembering his new tires.

Suddenly he was very excited. He could hardly wait to try his new tires out on the ride to the dig site.

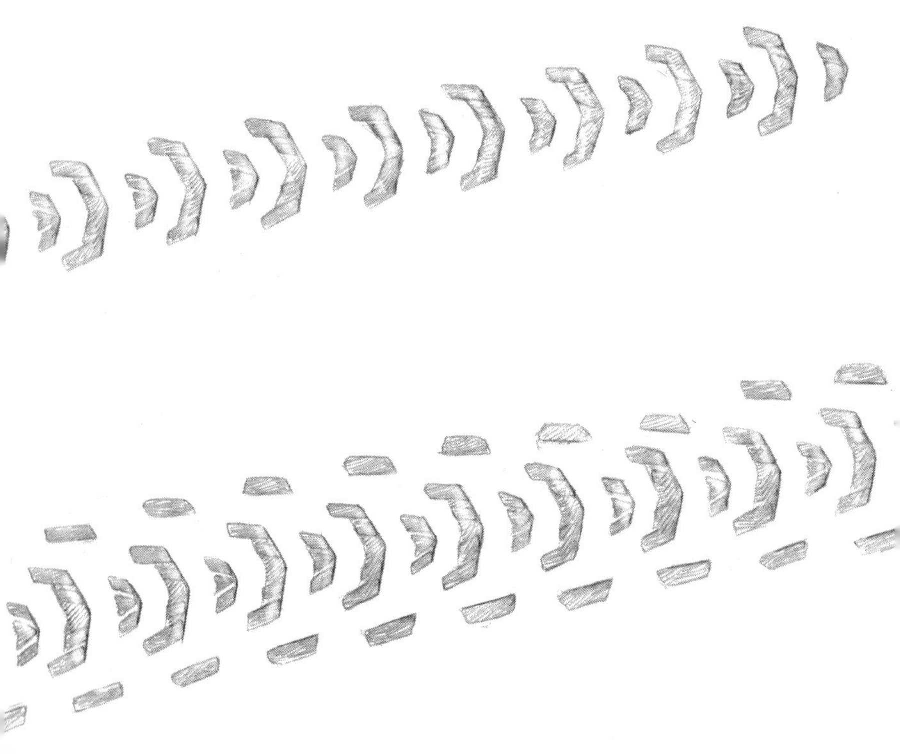

7

The new tires were great, there was no doubt about it. Fenton could hardly believe the difference. As he and Willy pedaled their way toward Sleeping Bear Mountain and the dig site, Fenton felt his bicycle crunch powerfully over the gravel and dirt.

And it was a good thing, too, because this time they had to make it all the way up the mountain by themselves.

Fenton glanced back at the rack on his bike. His box of colored pencils was securely strapped there, along with his latest dinosaur sketchbook. He hadn't used the sketchbook since that day in the museum in New York, the day he had found out that he was moving to Morgan. Now he was anxious to make some sketches of the footprints at the dig site, so he and Willy had stopped on their way and picked up Fenton's drawing supplies.

When they got to the dig site, they found Charlie by the tracks, his big dusty cowboy hat on his head and sweat dripping down his face.

"Well, howdy do, Fenton and Willy!" he bellowed, giving them a huge grin. "I'll bet you boys came up here to see the new print." He gestured toward the mound of rock he had been scraping at with a small pointy instrument.

"Wow," said Fenton, gazing at the mound, which was a few yards away from the first print. The two prints looked the same size, but this new one was still half covered with dirt and rock.

"Pretty impressive, huh?" said Charlie. "Thanks to this second print, we'll be able to get an idea of the animal's size."

"My dad said he was going to do some calculations on that today," said Fenton.

"That's right," said Charlie. "In fact, your father and Professor Martin are working on that right now, over in the trailer." He looked at Fenton and Willy and grinned. "You know, in the meanwhile, I could use some help uncovering this here track, if you boys feel like pitching in."

"Sure!" said Fenton excitedly.

"You bet!" said Willy.

The boys knelt down on the ground while Charlie showed them how to carefully scrape the surrounding dirt and rock from the footprint.

"Now, you have to be very gentle," he explained. "Remember, if you work too hard at it, you could end up scraping away part of the fossil itself."

For the next hour Charlie, Fenton, and Willy worked on the footprint together, using tiny picks, dental tools, toothbrushes, and even paintbrushes. Uncovering the fossil was harder than it looked, and Fenton couldn't believe how long it was taking. Still, the more they uncovered, the more excited he became.

Finally the entire footprint was exposed. Fenton stood up and stepped back, gazing at the two dinosaur prints with satisfaction. He could almost imagine the dinosaur itself taking that giant step in the mud a hundred million years ago. The problem was, he still didn't know exactly what kind of Cretaceous dinosaur had been doing the stepping.

Fenton walked over to where he had left his bicycle, unhooked the pad and pencils from his rack, and returned to the tracks.

"Well, what's that you've got there?" asked Charlie, looking over Fenton's shoulder. "You going to make a drawing?"

"This is one of my dinosaur sketchbooks," explained Fenton, flipping through the pages of drawings. "It always helps me understand dinosaurs better if I draw them, so I thought I'd make a sketch of these footprints."

"Good idea," said Charlie. "Looks like you've got some pretty impressive pictures in there, Fenton. Mind if I take a peek?"

Fenton handed him his sketchbook.

"Wow," said Willy, looking at the drawings as Charlie leafed through the sketchbook. "How'd you learn to draw dinosaurs so well, Fenton?"

Fenton shrugged. "I practice a lot."

"Well, Willy," said Charlie, taking off his hat and mopping his brow with his big hand, "what do you say you and I go back to the trailer and get a couple of cool drinks while Fenton does his drawings? We'll bring him back a soda or something."

"Sounds great," said Willy. "See you in a minute, Fenton."

But Fenton didn't answer. He was already completely involved in his sketching.

Drawing the footprints was a little different from drawing dinosaurs at the museum, but after a couple of tries, Fenton got the hang of it. In fact, since he himself had pitched in to help uncover the second print, Fenton felt as if he already knew every detail of it. As he sketched, he made note of the way the first toe on each foot was slightly smaller than the rest, almost as if it were a thumb, except on a foot instead of a hand.

By the time Willy and Charlie came back with the sodas, Fenton had made several drawings of the two footprints. Pleased with his work, he chugged down the cold soda they had brought him, excited to get back to his dinosaur books and start figuring out what kind of dinosaur had made the tracks.

Late that afternoon, Fenton lay on his bed, his nose buried in a thick book on dinosaurs, his sketchbook beside him. His room was still a mess from the day before; there were piles of clothes, games, and books everywhere.

Fenton knew that his mother probably wouldn't be too happy if she could see his room looking this way. It was funny, though—his father didn't seem to care much about things like clean rooms. In fact, Fenton's father didn't seem to notice a lot of the things that Fenton's mother had always paid attention to. For instance, right now Fenton was starting to feel a little hungry. He knew that if his mother were around she would probably be starting dinner about this time. But Fenton's father wasn't even back from the dig site yet.

Sighing, Fenton went back to his book. Maybe his father would come home soon and make something for them to eat. Meanwhile, he had all this information on Cretaceous dinosaurs to go through.

He had to admit, he was having a little more trouble coming up with the answer than he had expected. In fact, the more Fenton read, the more confused he got. Not only were there dozens of Cretaceous dinosaurs listed, but there were several facts about the footprint to keep straight too. Fenton knew he was looking for an Early-Cretaceous dinosaur with four toes on each of its back feet. But whenever he thought he had found it, something would turn out to be wrong.

For example, baryonyx, a dinosaur with huge claws and a long crocodile-shaped head, lived in the Early Cretaceous. It had huge feet—as big as the one that made the footprint. But so far the only baryonyx skeleton that had been discovered was found in England. So although it was possible, it didn't seem likely that an English baryonyx would have been walking around in Wyoming.

Tyrannosaurus rex skeletons had been found in Montana, which was right next door to Wyoming, but tyrannosaurus rex was way too big to leave a footprint the size of the ones at the dig site. Besides, it lived in the Late Cretaceous, not the Early Cretaceous.

The footprint could have been left by a nodosaurus, one of the four-footed, armor-coated dinosaurs Fenton had imagined drinking from the prehistoric lake that day at the dig site. Nodosaurus had four toes on its back feet, and pieces of its skeleton had even been found in Wyoming. But there really wasn't any way to tell for sure, especially without knowing whether the dinosaur that left the footprint was quadrupedal, like a nodosaurus, or bipedal.

Fenton closed his book, confused and disappointed. He had been sure he would know the answer by now. But there was just too much information to keep straight. He glanced at the T-rex alarm clock in the pile of pajamas on the floor. Maybe it was time to contact Max.

But the clock still hadn't been wound, so it still said ten minutes after eleven. That was another thing his mother would have taken care of if she were here! Frustrated, Fenton decided to take it downstairs and set it by the clock in the kitchen.

The stove clock said six o'clock. Fenton set his T-rex clock, winding the key in the back several times. As the clock started ticking and the T-rex head started bobbing to the rhythm of the gears inside, Fenton told himself that he would definitely try to remember to wind it every day from now on.

There were still fifteen minutes until it was time to contact Max, so Fenton decided to see what was in the refrigerator. Stomach growling, he opened the yellow door.

Fenton unwrapped the cold-cut packages. There was a little bit of turkey and a little bit of roast beef left, but not enough of either for a whole sandwich. Fenton sighed and closed the refrigerator. He was really getting sick of sandwiches.

And where was his father anyway? Shouldn't he have gone shopping by now and gotten them something else to eat? At home in New York, there had always been lots of stuff to snack on in the refrigerator.

Then Fenton got an idea—maybe he could order something in. Once in a while, in New York, his mother used to order in Chinese food for dinner. There must be a Chinese restaurant in Morgan that he could call. He felt funny about ordering food without permission, but after all, there was no one to ask right now, was there? Besides, this way he could surprise his father by having dinner waiting when he came home from the dig site.

He pulled the telephone book out of the shelf near the phone and began flipping through it. In the yellow pages he found what he was looking for under "R" for "Restaurants." "Peking Palace, Fine Chinese Cuisine," the advertisement read. Fenton picked up the phone.

"Peking Palace, good evening," answered a woman's voice.

"Yes, hello," said Fenton. "I'd like two egg rolls, and one large wonton soup, and—let's see—do you have chicken with cashew nuts?"

"Yes we do," said the woman. "We have a selection of Chinese specialties. We'll be happy to show you our menu when you arrive."

"No, but I'm not going there," explained Fenton. "I want to order in."

"Order in?"

"Yeah, you know," said Fenton. "I want you to deliver it."

"Deliver it?" repeated the woman. "Oh, no, we don't do that. You'll have to come pick it up."

"You don't deliver?" asked Fenton, astonished. "But isn't this a Chinese restaurant?"

"That's right," said the woman. "We have take-out, but you'll have to come and get it yourself."

Fenton thought a moment. He did have his bicycle. Maybe he could ride into town to pick up the food. "Okay," he said. "Where's the restaurant?"

"Right on the corner of Route 8 and Main," said the woman.

"Um, where's that exactly?" asked Fenton. "I'm new in Morgan."

"Oh, we're not in Morgan," said the woman. "We're in Fairpoint, about twenty miles down Route 8 from Morgan."

"Twenty miles!" said Fenton. That definitely sounded like way too far to ride. "Never mind, I'll call someplace else."

He hung up the phone and began to look through the phone book again. But there didn't seem to be any other Chinese restaurants listed.

This is ridiculous, he thought. In New York, there was practically a Chinese restaurant on every block! And they all delivered food to people's apartments. In fact, he couldn't remember ever having actually eaten Chinese food inside a Chinese restaurant. What kind of place was this? What were people supposed to do if they were hungry and didn't have anything to eat at home?

Fenton went back to the refrigerator. He'd just have to make do with the cold cuts. It looked like he could probably make half a turkey sandwich and half a roast-beef sandwich. Maybe if he toasted the bread it would taste a little different this time.

By the time he finished making his food, it was six-thirty, so he grabbed his plate and his T-rex clock and headed upstairs to the study and the computer. Putting the clock on the desk beside him, he took a bite of the roast-beef half, activated the modem, and keyed in Max's number.

CAN U REALLY
MAYBE

]HI MAX[

He typed, and waited, chewing.
Then came Max's response:

<HI FENTON. HOW R U?>

]THERES NO GOOD FOOD HERE. I CANT EVEN ORDER CHINESE[

<Y? WONT YOUR DAD LET U?>

]HES AT WORK. BUT CHINESE RESTAURANTS DONT DELIVER HERE[

<NO WAY!>

]NO KIDDING[

<WE HAD FRIED CHICKEN 2-NITE>

]LUCKY[

<TOO BAD U COULDNT COME 4 DINNER LIKE U USED 2>

]YEAH. ANYWAY I GUESS MY DAD WILL BE HOME SOON. THERES A NEW DINO FOOTPRINT AT THE DIG SITE. IM TRYING 2 FIGURE OUT WHAT KIND OF DINO, BUT THERES 2 MUCH INFORMATION 2 KEEP TRACK OF[

<U SHOULD USE THE COMPUTER>

]WHAT DO U MEAN? THERES NO COMPUTER PROGRAM 4 DINOSAURS IS THERE?[

<**WE CAN MAKE ONE**>

Fenton was excited. A computer program could be just the thing he needed to help him search through all that information on Cretaceous dinosaurs.

]CAN U REALLY DO THAT MAX?[

he typed in hopefully.

<**WHAT DO U NEED IT 2 DO?**>

Fenton explained the difficulties he was having to Max, who said it should be no problem designing a computer program that would help. For the next hour, the boys worked together on the program, Max showing Fenton how to set up a chart that would be able to record details about each dinosaur, including its size, when and where it lived, and how many toes it had.

]THIS IS GREAT MAX. THANKS[

typed Fenton when they were finished setting up the chart.

<**NOW ALL U HAVE 2 DO IS ENTER ALL THE INFORMATION ON ALL THE DINOSAURS. THEN ASK THE COMPUTER 2 FIND THE 1 U R LOOKING 4**>

explained Max.

Fenton was anxious to start entering the dinosaur information into the new computer program as soon as possible. But he figured he could fit in at least a game or two of Treasure Quest before signing off.

By the time he did sign off, the T-rex clock on the desk said eight twenty-five. The sun was just beginning to set, and Fenton's father still wasn't home from the dig site. Fenton wasn't worried, though. He knew how involved his father sometimes got in his work.

After hurrying up to his room to get his dinosaur books, Fenton settled himself in front of the computer again. In order to use the new computer program, he first had to enter the appropriate information—including the name of each dinosaur, when and where it lived, and the number of toes it had—for each of the Cretaceous dinosaurs in the books.

The time seemed to fly by on the T-rex clock as Fenton worked carefully to transfer the information from the books to the computer. It was a long, hard job, and Fenton could feel his eyelids growing heavy.

As the evening went on, and Fenton made his way through his dinosaur books, he began to feel sleepier and sleepier. Soon the words on the computer screen began to blur before his eyes. Eventually, a book still open on his lap, he put his head down on the desk in front of him and drifted off to sleep in the soft glow of the computer.

8

Fenton rolled over in bed and tried to stretch, wondering why his arms and legs felt so sore. He opened his eyes. The sun was streaming through the tiny windows along one wall of his room.

Suddenly he remembered—the computer! He must have fallen asleep in front of it last night. No wonder his body felt stiff and tired. But then how had he ended up in his bed?

Fenton got out of bed, rummaged through the clothes on his floor for a T-shirt and a pair of shorts, and headed downstairs. He found his father sitting on the couch, tying his shoes.

"Good morning, Fenton," said Mr. Rumplemayer. "Did you sleep all right?" He chuckled. "It looked like you were having quite a night there in front of the computer."

"Yeah, I was," said Fenton, sitting down next to his father. "When did you get home? How did I get in bed?"

Bill Rumplemayer smiled.

"I don't blame you for not remembering, son," he said. "You were pretty out of it when I came in and woke you up. I'm sorry I was so late. Professor Martin had to leave, so I stayed to finish those calculations on the stride length of the dinosaur."

Fenton perked up. "What did you come up with, Dad?" he asked. "Do you know how long the dinosaur was now?"

"Well, according to my calculations, depending on how fast it was moving, it must have been somewhere between fifteen and twenty-five feet long," said Mr. Rumplemayer.

"Wow, that's great," said Fenton. "Now the computer will definitely be able to figure out which dinosaur it was."

"The computer?"

"Max designed this great computer program for sorting out dinosaur information," Fenton explained. "That's what I was working on last night when I fell asleep. I'm almost done entering the information," Fenton told him.

"Well, it sounds like a very interesting program, son," said Fenton's father. "But I don't want you spending all your time indoors in front of the computer, either. Make sure you take some time to get outside and play a little." He stood up. "I'll see you later, I'm heading off to Sleeping Bear."

"But wait," said Fenton. "Don't you want to stay and hear what the computer has to say about which dinosaur made the footprints? I'm almost finished inputting the information, and I bet I'll have the answer pretty soon."

"I'd love to, Fenton, but I promised Charlie and Professor Martin I'd be out at the dig site early to look for more tracks," said his father. "We're hoping to figure out if this dinosaur was bipedal or quadrupedal. You know, the more information we can get, the closer we are to solving this mystery."

"Sure, Dad," said Fenton. "Bye." If his father didn't want to stick around and watch Max's computer program work, he would just have to miss out on the big moment when Fenton put it to the test. Once Fenton had found the answer, then his father would realize how great the program was.

Fenton climbed the stairs to the study and sat down in front of the computer. Finding his place in the dinosaur book he had been reading the night before, he settled down to finish his work.

Half an hour later, as he was getting near the end of the list of Cretaceous dinosaurs, he heard a voice call from outside.

"Fenton! Fenton, are you there?"

Fenton put down his book and stood up to look out the window. It was Willy.

Knocking on the glass to get Willy's attention, Fenton beckoned him inside. A moment later Willy was bounding up the stairs to the study.

"Hi, Fenton," he said, coming into the room and flopping down in the chair beside Fenton's. "Hey, wow, are you playing that computer game you were telling me about that your friend in New York made up—Search for Treasure, or whatever it's called?"

"Treasure Quest," corrected Fenton. "No, I'm not, but I am using another program that Max designed." He told Willy about the trouble he'd had sorting the information on Cretaceous dinosaurs, and how Max had suggested using the computer to figure it all out. "In fact, I'm just inputting my last dinosaur now," he said, typing in the last piece of information.

"Great," said Willy. "So that means the computer's ready to tell us which dinosaur made the tracks, right?"

"I hope so," said Fenton. "But first we have to tell it what to look for."

He keyed in the instructions the way Max had told him to, asking the computer to search the list of dinosaurs for one from the Early Cretaceous, with four toes, that was known to live in western North America—and adding the new information that it should be a dinosaur that was between fifteen and twenty-five feet long.

Fenton waited, crossing his fingers. After a few seconds, a word appeared on the screen.

]TENONTOSAURUS[

Fenton felt giddy with excitement. He looked at the computer screen again to be sure. Tenontosaurus was one of the dinosaurs that he had imagined in his scene of the Cretaceous that first day at the dig site—the one that had tried to use its massive tail to fight off the attacking pack of deinonychuses.

"What is it?" asked Willy, peering over his shoulder. "Did you find the answer?"

"I think so, Willy," said Fenton, grinning.

Indeed, tenontosaurus fit the description perfectly. A plant eater with a strong, thick tail, tenontosaurus had four toes on each back foot. One toe was even slightly smaller than the rest, the way Fenton had noticed in the footprints when he was sketching them that day. The dinosaur grew to lengths of fifteen to twenty-two feet and had been found in western North America.

"Here," he said, leafing through one of the books to locate a picture of tenontosaurus for Willy. "It seems like this is who we've been looking for."

He handed the book to Willy.

"Tenontosaurus," read Willy.

"That's right," said Fenton happily.

"So I guess this dinosaur is quad— quadru—" Willy tried, looking at the drawing in the book. It showed the dinosaur standing on all four legs, chewing a leaf.

"Quadrupedal," said Fenton, taking the book back from Willy and examining the picture. "Actually, it probably did walk on all four legs most of the time, but it could also run on its back two legs if it had to move fast."

He smiled, thinking about how his father and the others

were out searching for another footprint at this very moment, trying to determine whether the dinosaur that made the tracks had been bipedal or quadrupedal—and meanwhile, he and Willy had all the information right here in front of them.

"Come on," he said, shutting the book suddenly, "we'd better get out to the dig site and tell everyone else the good news!"

"Dad! Charlie! Professor Martin!" Fenton called, still out of breath from the bike ride up Sleeping Bear Mountain Road. "I found it! I found it! I know the answer!"

He jumped off his bike and ran, stumbling over rocks, towards the area where the footprints were. But to his surprise, none of the paleontologists were nearby. He looked back toward the camp and saw his father, Lily Martin, and Charlie near one of the trailers. His father and Professor Martin were sitting on folding lawn chairs, drinking cans of soda, and Charlie was standing over what looked like a barbecue.

"Dad! Dad!" yelled Fenton excitedly, running toward the trailer, with Willy close behind him.

"Oh, hello, son," said Mr. Rumplemayer quietly. "Hello, Willy."

"You boys are just in time for lunch," said Charlie. "I'm making up some of my world-famous barbecued ribs."

"Goodness knows we could use a hearty meal after the morning we've had!" sighed Professor Martin, taking off her hat and fanning herself with it.

"We've had a bit of a bad time with the footprints," explained Fenton's father. "We thought we had it all figured out, but—"

"But that's what I came to tell you, Dad," said Fenton happily. "I've got the answer! I know what kind of dinosaur made the prints."

"Fenton looked it up on the computer," added Willy.

Fenton looked excitedly at his father, Charlie, and Professor Martin. He couldn't understand why none of them seemed to be interested in what he had to say. Even Charlie was busy brushing barbecue sauce on the ribs.

"Fenton, before you get all worked up about this, there's something you should know," said his father. "We found another footprint this morning—"

"You did?" Fenton burst in happily. "That's great! Why didn't you tell me sooner? Come on, Willy, let's go look at it!"

He grabbed Willy and ran toward the track site as fast as he could, only vaguely aware that his father was still saying something behind him.

Fenton looked down at the reddish ground and saw the two large hind footprints that he already knew about. And there, a few yards ahead of the second print, rising out of the dirt, was a third foot-shaped lump—this one much smaller than the other two.

Fenton moved closer to examine it.

"Look at how much smaller it is than the other two," he

said to Willy, brushing away some of the dirt. "It must be from one of the dinosaur's front feet."

"Yes, and that's exactly the problem," said a voice behind them.

Fenton turned and saw Charlie standing nearby, a barbecue fork in one hand and a pot holder in the other.

"What do you mean—problem?" asked Fenton. "There's no problem at all. That's what I keep trying to explain to everybody. I worked the whole thing out on the computer. This must just be the print of one of the front feet of the tenonto—"

He stopped short.

He looked at the new print again. Suddenly he saw just what was wrong with it. He counted again to be sure. It was true, all right—this print showed only three toes. Everybody knew that tenontosaurus had five toes on each of its front feet.

"But that doesn't make sense," he said quietly, wrinkling his forehead.

"Now you know how the rest of us feel," said Charlie sympathetically. "We've been trying to figure it out all morning. Come on, you look like you could use some of my special ribs about now."

"What's wrong?" asked Willy as he and Fenton followed Charlie back to the trailer. "Isn't tenontosaurus the right answer?"

Fenton sighed dejectedly. "The front print doesn't have the right number of toes for it to be a tenontosaurus."

"That's what has us all so confused," said Charlie as he headed toward the barbecue.

Fenton took a seat near his father. "I was so sure it was a tenontosaurus," he said.

"I know," said Lily Martin, shaking her head slowly. "Tenontosaurus was my prime suspect too, Fenton. But with this new print it just doesn't make sense."

"It's a real mystery," agreed Fenton's father.

"But if it's not tenontosaurus, can't the computer just tell us what kind of dinosaur it really was, Fenton?" asked Willy.

Fenton brightened. Of course, the computer would be able to help them.

"Sure," he said. "I mean, so we were wrong about tenontosaurus. That just means the tracks must be from another Cretaceous dinosaur, right? I'm sure it'll be no problem for the computer to figure out which one."

"Computer?" asked Charlie, handing Fenton a paper plate of ribs.

"Fenton's friend in New York helped him design a program to organize dinosaur information," Mr. Rumplemayer explained. He turned to his son. "But Fenton, I don't know if the computer's going to be able to help you here. You see, it's not really that simple—"

"For Fenton it is," boasted Willy, cutting him off. "Just you wait and see. Fenton'll have the right answer in no time!"

But suddenly Fenton wasn't so sure. He had just realized

exactly what it was about this new three-toed print that had his father and the others so concerned. And the more he thought about it, the less certain he was that the computer program was going to be able to find the answer.

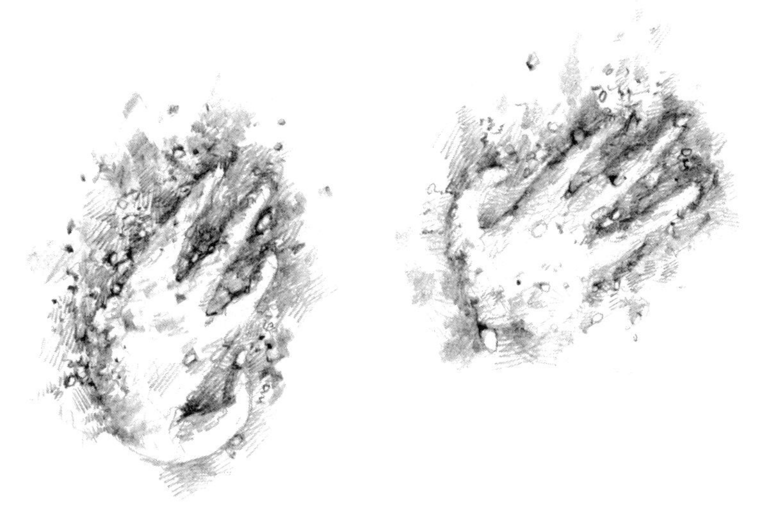

9

The problem with the three-toed print was this: Fenton couldn't think of a dinosaur that could possibly have made it.

After all, he reasoned as he and Willy rode their bikes back down the mountain toward home after lunch, he had already asked the computer to search for every known Early-Cretaceous dinosaur of the right size, from the right area, with four toes on each of its back feet.

And the computer had come up with only one—tenontosaurus.

That meant tenontosaurus was the only dinosaur that fit the description. But it couldn't have been tenontosaurus, because tenontosaurus had five toes on its front feet, and whatever dinosaur made these tracks had only three.

Fenton knew there had to be a logical explanation for all this. He just had to go back to the computer and recheck his information.

"Listen, Willy," he said as they rode up the dirt road toward home. "I think I probably have to do some more work on the dinosaur program before the computer can give us the answer."

"What do you mean?" asked Willy.

"Well, right now, the only dinosaur that the computer says could have made those tracks is tenontosaurus," Fenton explained. "But we know that can't be right. The problem is, if I ask the computer to search for a dinosaur that fits the tenontosaurus description but has only three toes on its front feet, it won't be able to come up with anything at all."

"Are you telling me that it wasn't a dinosaur that made those tracks?" asked Willy as they approached Fenton's driveway.

"No, no, I'm sure it was a dinosaur," answered Fenton. "But maybe I made a mistake when I was entering all the original dinosaur information into the computer. You know, I might have listed the number of toes wrong for one of the dinosaurs I put into the program, or something." He sighed. "Anyway, I'm going to have to go over every bit of information I put into the computer."

"You want me to help?" asked Willy.

"No, I guess there isn't really anything you can do," Fenton told him, heading up the driveway toward home. "It's up to me and the computer now. But thanks."

"Okay, good luck!" called Willy, pedaling down the road toward his own house. "I'll stop by later and see how you're doing!"

Fenton spent the rest of the day going over every single piece of dinosaur information he had put into the computer. He checked every fact on the computer's dinosaur chart against at least two of his dinosaur books. But at six-thirty he still hadn't found the problem.

He decided to exit the dinosaur program and contact Max. After all, it was Max's program. Maybe he could figure out what had gone wrong.

]MAX ITS ME. R U THERE?[

<**HI FENTON. SORRY BUT I CANT REALLY PLAY TQ RIGHT NOW. I HAVE 2 GO 2 THE GOOD-BYE PARTY IN THE LOBBY FOR GUS**>

]ACTUALLY I CANT PLAY NOW EITHER. IM WORKING ON THE DINO COMPUTER PROGRAM. BUT I HAVE A QUESTION ABOUT IT[

<**WHATS UP?**>

]COULD IT MAKE A MISTAKE MAYBE?[

<**U MEAN FINDING THE DINOSAUR YOURE ASKING IT 4?**>

]RIGHT[

<**NO WAY. NOT UNLESS U MADE A MISTAKE IN-PUTTING THE ORIGINAL INFORMATION**>

]THATS DEFINITELY NOT IT. IVE BEEN OVER THE IN-

FORMATION + THERE R NO MISTAKES AT ALL[

<COMPUTERS DONT MAKE MISTAKES, ONLY PEOPLE DO. U MUST HAVE MISSED SOMETHING. LISTEN, I HAVE 2 GO. THE PARTYS STARTING DOWNSTAIRS>

]OK MAX. THANKS ANYWAY. SAY BYE 2 GUS 4 ME[

<TALK 2 U SOON>

Fenton signed off, disappointed. He had been hoping that Max would be able to solve the problem for him. But apparently, the trouble wasn't with the computer. There must be something else he wasn't thinking of.

He sighed. Somehow he just couldn't bring himself to run the dinosaur program again. He had been going through it all day, and he couldn't stand the idea of looking at it anymore. He couldn't help wishing that he was in New York, at Gus's goodbye party, or anywhere but here staring at the computer screen.

Just then he heard a shout from outside. Pushing open the study window, he stuck his head out.

It was Willy.

"Hi, Fenton. Any luck with the computer?"

"None at all," said Fenton. "I just can't figure out what the problem is."

"That's too bad," said Willy. "Listen, do you want to come over for dinner tonight?"

"To your house?"

"Sure," said Willy. "My mom and dad said I could invite you."

Fenton thought a moment. It was already almost seven o'clock, and his father hadn't come home from the dig site. It was still light out, so his father might not be back for quite a while. He might even work really late, as he had the night before. Fenton was sure his father hadn't planned anything for dinner.

"Okay," he said. "I'll be right down."

"We're having spaghetti and meatballs," said Willy when Fenton got outside.

"Mmm," said Fenton, feeling his stomach growl, "my favorite." Suddenly, he missed his mother. Spaghetti had been one of her specialties back in New York. It sure felt like a long time since he'd had a real dinner, the kind his mother used to make. It seemed like all he and his father ever ate for dinner in Wyoming was sandwiches.

The boys made their way along the path behind the house through the pine trees, past the clearing with the clubhouse shack, and on to Willy's house. A little girl was playing outside, dragging a bit of string around for a tiny orange kitten to chase.

"Dad was looking for you, Willy," she said. "You better go in, you might be in trouble."

"That's my little sister, Jane," said Willy, leading Fenton past her toward the house. "Don't listen to anything she says."

"I am not little!" said Jane, dropping her string and putting her hands on her hips. "I'm already five and three quarters."

"Oh, I forgot, you're a real old lady, Jane," said Willy, winking at Fenton. "Or should I call you Grandma from now on?"

"Mom! Dad!" Jane called. "Willy's being mean to me again!"

"Willy," came a man's voice from inside the house, "stop teasing your sister."

"Come on, let's go inside," said Willy to Fenton as Jane stuck out her tongue.

Willy pulled open the screen door and the boys stepped into the kitchen, where a man stood stirring a pot on the stove and a woman was grating cheese into a bowl at one of the counters.

"Mom, Dad, this is my friend Fenton," said Willy.

The woman turned from the counter and smiled. "Fenton, it's very nice to meet you," she said.

"Hello, Fenton," said the man, grinning from his spot near the stove.

"Hi, Mr. and Mrs. Whitefox," said Fenton. "Thanks for inviting me for dinner."

"Our pleasure, Fenton," said Willy's father, going back to his stirring.

"Yes," said Willy's mother. "I'm just so glad that someone around Willy's age has moved in nearby."

"Now, what do you say we put you boys to work," said Mr.

Whitefox. "Willy, there's some lettuce in the refrigerator that needs to be washed for a salad. Fenton, maybe you can go outside and tell Jane to come in and set the table."

"Okay," said Fenton, stepping back out through the screen door. He was glad he hadn't gotten the lettuce-washing job. He had never washed lettuce before. He wasn't even sure how you did it. Did you use soap? Probably not. Come to think of it, he remembered his mother washing lettuce in their kitchen back in New York. She just rinsed it under water and then put it in a special spinning thing to dry it. Fenton wondered if the Whitefoxes had one of those lettuce spinners and if Willy knew how to use it.

He found Willy's little sister in the backyard, still playing with the kitten.

"Jane," he said. "Your dad says to tell you to set the table."

Jane made a face. "I hate chores," she whined.

"Come on," said Fenton, "I'll help you do it."

"Okay," said Jane, scooping the orange kitten up into her arms. She looked at Fenton. "Hey, what's your name, anyway?"

"Fenton Rumplemayer. I live next door in the white house."

"Oh," said Jane. She held out the cat toward him. "Do you want to pet Simonetta?"

"Sure," said Fenton, reaching out to stroke the kitten's soft fur. "Simonetta—what kind of a name is that?"

"Well," explained Jane, "at first her name was Simon, but

then we found out that she was a girl, so I changed it to Simonetta."

Fenton laughed. "Come on," he said, "we'd better go inside."

Jane and Fenton collected the plates, napkins, and silverware from the kitchen, and she led him into the dining room. Five minutes later the table was set and everyone was seated.

"Fenkon helped me set the table," said Jane.

"Uh—that's Fenton," Fenton corrected quietly.

"Fenkon is my new friend," Jane went on.

"His name's Fenton, you ninny," said Willy. "And anyway, he's my friend, not yours."

"Willy, stop teasing your sister," said Mrs. Whitefox.

"Well, I get the feeling that Fenton is going to be a friend of the whole Whitefox family," said Mr. Whitefox.

"Don't listen to my sister," said Willy under his breath. "She always tries to copy me."

The Whitefoxes passed the serving dishes of food around the table, and soon Fenton's plate was filled. He looked down at the big pile of spaghetti, warm piece of buttered bread, and serving of cool, crisp salad in front of him.

"Wow," he said appreciatively, "this looks as good as one of my mom's dinners."

Mr. Whitefox grinned.

"Enjoy it, Fenton," he said.

"I'd love to meet your mother, Fenton," said Mrs. Whitefox. "There are so few people who live this far out of town, and it's always nice to get to know new neighbors. Perhaps we can invite your parents to dinner sometime soon."

"Well, actually, I don't think my mom would be able to make it," said Fenton. "You see, she's in India."

"India, my goodness," said Mrs. Whitefox. "That's pretty far away."

"Yeah," said Fenton. "She's working over there for a year. But I'm sure my father would like to come sometime." He's bound to get sick of sandwiches pretty soon, thought Fenton.

"What kind of work is your mother doing in India, Fenton?" asked Mrs. Whitefox.

"She's studying dinosaurs," Fenton told her.

"Fenton's father studies dinosaurs too," said Willy. "Over at Sleeping Bear."

"There's no such thing as dinosaurs," said Jane. "They were only made up to scare people."

"That's not true!" said Willy indignantly.

"Jane, honey, I think you're thinking of dragons, not dinosaurs," said Mr. Whitefox gently. "It's dragons that are pretend, not dinosaurs."

"Oh," said Jane, looking worried. "So dinosaurs *are* real?"

"All the dinosaurs are dead now, though, Jane," Fenton reassured her. "They can't hurt you because they're not alive anymore."

Jane gazed gratefully at Fenton.

"What a ninny," said Willy under his breath, earning a sharp look from his father.

By the time dinner was over, Fenton was stuffed. He'd had three big servings of spaghetti and four pieces of bread. He had even helped himself to a second helping of salad. And somehow he had managed to force down a piece of homemade banana cake for dessert. Fenton hadn't eaten a dinner that delicious since he had left New York.

"Thanks so much, Mr. and Mrs. Whitefox," he said after he and Willy had helped clear the dishes. "That was really great."

"You're welcome anytime, Fenton," said Willy's father, smiling.

"Next time maybe you can bring your father, too," said Willy's mother.

"See you tomorrow, Fenton," said Willy.

"Sure," said Fenton, heading out the screen door into the darkness. "Come on over when you get up."

"Bye, Fenkon!" called Jane, peering out the screen door and waving.

"Bye, Jane," he called back, laughing.

As Fenton made his way along the path through the pine trees, he was surprised by how easy it was to see where he was going, even though the sun had gone down.

Looking up at the sky, he was amazed by what he saw. There were more stars up there than he had ever seen in his life. There must be millions and millions of them—so many that they were practically touching each other. The entire sky was filled with their hazy white light. Fenton had never seen anything like it before—even the star show at the planetarium next door to the museum in New York hadn't been this amazing. Besides, thought Fenton, the stars on the planetarium ceiling were really just lights projected on the ceiling to look like stars—these stars above him now were the real thing.

As Fenton approached his house, he could see that the living-room lights were on. His father must be home from work. Fenton quickened his steps, anxious to get inside and find out if there was any news from the dig site.

But when he opened the door and stepped into the living room, he was completely surprised by the stern look on his father's face.

"Fenton!" said Mr. Rumplemayer. "Where on earth have you been?"

"What do you mean? I went to Willy's for dinner."

"Willy's!" repeated his father angrily. "Fenton, do you realize that I had no idea where you were? Do know how worried I was?"

"Sorry, Dad," said Fenton, shrugging. After all, he hadn't even known when his father would get home from work. Going to Willy's for dinner had seemed like a smart idea.

"Sorry? What makes you think you can just run off to Willy's like that without telling me?" Mr. Rumplemayer

demanded, his face growing redder by the second.

Fenton stared at his father.

"But Dad, you weren't even here for me to tell!" he said impatiently.

"Well, in that case you leave me a note or something," said his father. "You know better than to just run off like that!" He shook his head. "I can't understand why you would think that things would be different now, just because we're in Wyoming instead of New York."

"What are you talking about, Dad?" said Fenton, angry now. "Everything's different here! Nothing's the way it was in New York, don't you see?!"

"No, I don't see, Fenton," said Mr. Rumplemayer, folding his arms across his chest. "What I do see is this—I see that just because your mother's not around, you think you can get away with coming and going whenever you want!"

Fenton was furious. How could his father say something like that when that was exactly how *he* had been acting lately?

"Listen, Dad," he said, his voice getting louder. "At least when Mom's around, she's actually *around*, instead of staying at work all night like you do! At least when Mom's around, I don't have to eat sandwiches all the time, and I know that we're going to have dinner!" He took a deep breath. "At least when Mom's around, I know someone cares about me!"

Fenton turned from his father and ran out of the room. As fast as he could, he climbed the stairs to the second floor and scrambled up the ladder to his room.

The room was a mess, and suddenly Fenton couldn't stand it that way anymore. Fuming, he stormed around the attic, folding his clothes and putting them into his dresser drawers. His father just wasn't being fair, he thought angrily, stacking his games on a shelf in his closet. Why did he have to be so mean?

By the time Fenton was finished with his room, he was exhausted. Everything was unpacked, and the empty boxes were stacked against a wall. He had even put his dinosaur sheets on his bed.

Turning out the light, Fenton climbed into bed. He was still angry at his father, but he was too tired even to think about it anymore.

In five minutes he was asleep.

10

"Fenton," said the voice softly. "Fenton, wake up." Fenton was dimly aware of a hand gently shaking his shoulder.

"Wake up," the voice said again. "Wake up, son."

Fenton opened his eyes and saw his father's face.

"Dad," he mumbled, closing his eyes again and rolling over.

"Wake up, son. I'd like to talk to you about last night," said his father.

Suddenly Fenton remembered—the night before, the argument. He opened his eyes and looked at his father.

"Son, I was wrong," said Mr. Rumplemayer.

Fenton sat up in bed. "Dad?"

"I was wrong to get so angry at you last night," his father went on. "Sure, I was worried, but I also realize that a lot of what you said was true. Things have been different here in Wyoming, without your mother around, and I know I probably haven't been acting like much of a parent lately."

"I know you're busy, Dad," said Fenton. "And I know I should have left you a note that I was going to Willy's. But it seems like you're never around at all."

"I've got a lot of work out at the dig site, son," said his father. "But how about this—I'll do my best to get home on time more often. And I'll try to make sure there's food around the house for when I'm not here."

"Maybe we can cook together sometimes, too, Dad," said Fenton, thinking of the way the whole family had pitched in at the Whitefoxes' the night before.

"That would be great," said his father. "It's going to be a lot harder for us without your mother around, but maybe if we work together we can manage some of the things she used to do. I'm not much of a cook, but I'm willing to try if you are."

"Sure, Dad," said Fenton. "Maybe we can even ask Mom how to make spaghetti the next time we talk to her."

"That sounds like a good idea," said Mr. Rumplemayer, smiling. He stood up. "Now, what do you say we start with breakfast? Maybe we can drive into town and look for a store. I'm pretty sure I remember how to scramble an egg."

"I know where there's a store," said Fenton, climbing out of bed. "The Morgan Market. I saw it the day we arrived."

"Okay, then, the Morgan Market it is," said Mr. Rumplemayer. "As soon as you're dressed, we'll go."

An hour later Fenton and his father were finishing their breakfast—toast, scrambled eggs, and orange juice.

"Well, that was delicious," said Fenton's father. "I'll tell you, I was starting to get pretty sick of sandwiches."

"Me too," said Fenton, laughing. "I never want to see another turkey or roast-beef sandwich in my life!"

"I'd better head out to the dig site," said Mr. Rumplemayer, standing. "Maybe we can find something to help clear up the mystery of those tracks."

"Okay, Dad, bye," said Fenton. "Good luck."

Well, I guess I'd better head back to the computer and see if I can figure out what went wrong, thought Fenton. But after the frustrations of the night before, he didn't have much hope left.

As he sat down in front of the computer in the second-floor office, something caught his eye. A piece of paper was sticking out of the top of the FAX machine on the desk. He reached over and pulled it out, recognizing the handwriting immediately—it was a letter from his mother!

Fenton took the letter upstairs to his room and lay down on his bed to read it.

Dear Fenton,

Hi, honey, how are you? I am sending this FAX from my hotel in Delhi before checking out to catch the train to the village of Kapoor, where I hear there have been some interesting fossil discoveries.

Yesterday I went for a walk in the city. I stopped in a bank to exchange some American money (Indian money is called rupees and looks very different from our dollars). Standing on line with me was a woman with her two children. The girl looked about your age or a bit older, and the little boy was probably only about one or two years old. He reminded me of you when you were that age—he has the same big, round eyes you had.

Whenever the woman moved forward on line, the little boy would clutch on to her clothing as if he were afraid that she was going to leave him. It made me think of the way you were when you were just a baby. Everywhere I went, you would toddle after me, never letting me out of your sight. Sometimes I practically found myself tripping over you! But then how independent you became as you got older—like that day at the museum when you were four, when you wandered off to see the coelophysis all by yourself!

Well, I guess I'd better go now. My train will be leaving soon. I'll call or write again soon to tell you all about Kapoor. Meanwhile, please try to help your father out when you can. He's not used to running the household on his own.

I miss you and send you a big hug.

Love,

Mom

Fenton read the letter again. He was surprised that his mother still hadn't mentioned any tigers. And it was funny, the stuff she'd said about how he used to follow her around. Fenton couldn't imagine himself doing something like that. But he supposed all babies must do it.

His eyes traveled to the maiasaur paperweight on the shelf below the window. The glass dome reflected the sunlight that streamed into the room.

Then he had a thought. The thought turned into an idea, and suddenly, he was so excited that he leaped off his bed and hurried down the ladder to the office as fast as he could.

Flipping through his sketchbook, he located the drawings of the footprints he had made at Sleeping Bear. He quickly sketched in the new, smaller print as he remembered it, with its three toes, and held the drawing at arm's length to examine it. It was definitely a possibility. Now he just had to check a couple of other things to be sure.

He flipped through the nearest dinosaur book for a picture of tenontosaurus. Finding one, he examined the toes on the back feet carefully. They looked just as he had remembered them—three regular-sized toes and a fourth, smaller toe, almost like a thumb.

Slamming the book shut, he raced back downstairs and out to the garage. Hurrying over to his bicycle, which was leaning against the far wall, he bent over to examine the tires. No good—the rubber was patterned only in the center of the tire, and not at all on the edges. Willy's was really the bike he had to look at. Besides, he needed two people in order try out his idea.

Fenton ran as fast as he could down the path through the pine trees to Willy's.

"Willy! Willy!" he called as he approached the yellow house. "Come quick!"

Mrs. Whitefox poked her head out the kitchen door.

"Oh, hello, Fenton," she said. "Is everything all right? Would you like some breakfast?"

"Yes, no, I mean everything's fine, and no breakfast, thanks," said Fenton panting. "But I need to see Willy. Is he here?"

"Hi, Fenton," said Willy, appearing next to his mother at the screen door. "What's up?"

"I need your help with something right away," said Fenton. "Where's your bike?"

"In the garage," said Willy, coming outside. "I'll get it."

A moment later Willy appeared with his bicycle.

"Okay," said Fenton, "now we need water. Do you have a hose?"

"Of course we have a hose, Fenton. What's this all about? Are you going to wash my bike or something?"

"Hi, Fenkon," said Jane shyly, coming outside.

"Hi, Jane," said Fenton quickly. "Hurry, Willy, we need to make a puddle!"

"Okay," said Willy, rolling his eyes, "but I want you to

know that this isn't making any sense to me at all." He walked around the corner of the house and reappeared, dragging behind him a long green hose with a thin stream of water coming from it.

A minute later they had made a large mud puddle in a dusty patch near the house.

"Ick," said Jane, wrinkling her nose at the mud. "Yucky!"

"Now," directed Fenton, "Willy, ride through the puddle on your bike."

Willy sighed. "Fenton, is this about my bike tracks again?" he asked. "Because if it is, I already told you—"

"Just do it, okay, Willy?" pleaded Fenton. "I want to check something."

"Oh, all right," said Willy, hopping on his bike.

Fenton watched as Willy rode his bike though the puddle and back again.

"Okay," said Fenton. "Now ride me on the bike through the puddle, the way you did the day my bike was at the shop."

"Sure," said Willy, shrugging. "But I still don't see what this is all about."

Jane giggled as Fenton climbed up on the seat behind Willy.

"I want a ride too," she said. "Can I be next?"

The boys managed to balance together on the bike, and Willy pedaled it through the puddle again.

"Okay," said Fenton, hopping off the bike and hurrying over to inspect the puddle. "Now let's see what happened."

He examined the thick tire tracks in the mud as Willy came to stand by his side.

"There!" said Fenton, pointing triumphantly.

Just as he had expected, there were two different kinds of tire tracks in the mud. The first one showed the simple V-shaped pattern that Willy had said his bike usually made. But the second track, the one from when the two boys had ridden together, showed both the V-shaped pattern and the dotted-line pattern from the edges of the tires.

"Wow," said Willy, amazed. "Look at that! It's just like that day in front of Mrs. Wadsworth's!"

"Come on," said Fenton. "Now we've got to get back to my house and get my bike too."

"Why?" asked Willy. "Are we going to do the experiment on your tires?"

"No need to," said Fenton. "We've got all the evidence we need right here. But we do have to ride out to the dig site right away."

"How come?" asked Willy, still bewildered.

"Because," said Fenton, "I think I just discovered the key to the mystery of the footprints!"

11

"Dad, listen to me," said Fenton. "This time I really think I've solved it."

Fenton and Willy had arrived at the dig site out of breath and had found Bill Rumplemayer, Charlie Smalls, and Lily Martin squatting by the dinosaur tracks.

"Okay, Fenton," said Mr. Rumplemayer, "go ahead and tell us your idea."

"Why not?" said Charlie, grinning. "It's bound to be at least as good as what we've come up with—which is absolutely nothing!" He laughed.

"Yes, Fenton, I'm interested to hear what it is you have in mind," said Professor Martin.

"Me too," said Willy. "What's this all about, anyway?"

"Well," Fenton began, "the problem with these tracks is that no known dinosaur could possibly have made them."

The others nodded.

"From everything we know," Fenton went on, "it seems as though these footprints were made by an Early-Cretaceous dinosaur between fifteen and twenty-five feet long, with four toes on its back feet and three on its front. But that description doesn't fit any of the dinosaurs known to live during that time period in this area."

"Yup, that's it in a nutshell, Fenton," agreed Charlie.

"Unfortunately," added Professor Martin.

"But there is one dinosaur that fits the description in every way except for the number of toes on the front feet, and that's tenontosaurus," said Fenton. "Tenontosaurus lived in western North America during the Early Cretaceous, and it grew to be fifteen to twenty-two feet long. It had four toes on each hind foot, and one of them was even a little smaller than the rest, the way it looks in these two big prints here. So my guess is, we can be pretty sure that a tenontosaurus did leave those two back prints after all."

"I'm with you so far, son," said Mr. Rumplemayer. "But then how do you explain that three-toed front print?"

"Yeah," said Willy. "I still don't get it. You said tenontosaurus had five front toes. What happened to the other two?"

"Well," said Fenton, looking at them all and grinning, "what if the tenontosaurus that made the two back prints isn't the same tenontosaurus that made the smaller print in front?"

"What do you mean?" asked Professor Martin.

"Maybe the two bigger prints were made by a full-grown tenontosaurus walking on its hind legs," said Fenton.

"Tenontosaurus did have a habit of walking upright on two legs when it was moving quickly," said Charlie, nodding.

"And maybe the smaller print in front of it was made by a smaller tenontosaurus that was also walking on its hind legs," said Fenton.

"You mean that smaller print isn't from the dinosaur's front foot?" said Willy.

Fenton nodded. "I think it's from a smaller tenontosaurus that was following the larger one. After all, just because that smaller print looks like it's in front of the larger ones doesn't mean that it had to be made first. The small dinosaur could have been walking behind the big one."

"It's a good idea, but unfortunately it still doesn't really work," said Professor Martin. "If a young tenontosaurus had made that small print with its back foot, it would have left four toe marks, like the adult did. The small print has only three toe marks."

"I'm afraid Professor Martin is right, Fenton," said Mr. Rumplemayer. "Your theory still doesn't explain why the smaller tenontosaurus would leave a three-toed print. It would have had four back toes, just like an adult."

"Nice try, Fenton," said Charlie.

"But wait!" said Fenton excitedly. "I have an explanation for that, too. I figured it out from Willy's bike!"

"Huh?" said Willy.

"From a bicycle?" asked Professor Martin.

"This I gotta hear," said Charlie.

"All right," said Fenton. "We all know that one of

tenontosaurus's back toes is smaller than the other three, like a thumb."

Everyone nodded.

"So my idea is this," said Fenton. "Maybe the baby dinosaur was so lightweight that the smaller toe on the side of its foot wasn't being pressed hard enough into the ground to make a mark."

"Hey!" said Willy. "I get it! Like with my bike!"

"Right," said Fenton, grinning and walking over to pick Willy's bicycle up off the ground nearby.

"You see," said Fenton, pointing at the pattern in the tires of the bicycle, "when Willy rides his bike alone, only the center of this tire pattern—the part with the V's in it—leaves a track. But when he rides with me on the bike too, this part of the tire—the part with the dotted-line pattern on the outer edge—shows also. That's because the bike weighs a lot more with both of us on it, so the tires are pushed deeper into the ground, which gives the edges of the tires a chance to make a mark too instead of just the center."

For a moment no one said anything. They were all too busy thinking.

Then Charlie started to laugh.

"Well, I'll be!" he said. "I think you might just have something there, Fenton!"

"It certainly sounds like a plausible explanation," agreed Professor Martin.

"Wow," said Willy appreciatively.

"Very nice work, son," said Mr. Rumplemayer, beaming.

Fenton looked at them all and grinned. There had never really been any doubt in his mind that he would be able to solve the mystery. It had just taken a little time.

And Max had been right—the problem hadn't been with the computer program at all. Fenton couldn't wait until six-thirty to modem Max and tell him all about it.

One morning two weeks later, Fenton sat in the yellow kitchen, talking on the phone to his mother in Kapoor, India.

"Okay, Mom," he said as he wrote on the index card in front of him, "first chop up the onions and garlic for the sauce and put them in the pot with the oil. I got that. Then what do we do next?"

Fenton wrote quickly as his mother gave him the rest of the instructions.

"And finally, you simmer the sauce for about an hour," his mother finished. "But you know, Fenton, you could just go buy a jar of tomato sauce from the store and use that on the spaghetti if you want to make things a little easier."

"Is that what you do, Mom?"

"Well, no," his mother said. "I like to make my own sauce."

"Then that's what Dad and I want to do, too," said Fenton.

"I'm so proud of the way you're helping your father manage things, Fenton," said his mother. "Imagine, first you helped him solve that mystery out at the dig site, and now you're helping him make dinner!" She laughed.

"Nothing to it, Mom," said Fenton proudly.

"Well, now that you two have decided to become gourmet cooks, maybe I should write down some more of my favorite recipes and send them to you," said Mrs. Rumplemayer. "That way you won't have to call me long distance when you want to have a dinner party."

Fenton laughed.

"Sounds like a good idea, Mom," he said. "Well, I guess I'd better go so Dad and I can head over to the Morgan Market and pick up these ingredients."

By six o'clock that evening, the spaghetti was ready and their dinner guests had arrived. Fenton, his father, Willy, Charlie, and Lily Martin sat around the big table in the dining room.

"Well, Fenton," said Charlie, helping himself to some spaghetti, "now that we've uncovered more footprints, it definitely looks like you were right—there *were* two different tenontosauruses."

"And we can be pretty sure from the way the smaller tracks weave in and out among the larger ones that the baby dinosaur was following the adult one," added Professor Martin.

"Yup, it was probably just toddling along after its mommy or daddy," said Charlie, grinning.

Fenton smiled, remembering what his mother had said in

her letter about the way he had once followed her around. It was kind of fun to think that he and a tenontosaurus had acted the same way when they were babies.

He thought about what they must have looked like, the adult tenontosaurus and its baby, running on their hind legs through the mud of the Cretaceous, and he wondered what they had been running from. Maybe it was a pack of deinonychuses after all, he thought, remembering the scene he had imagined that day at the dig site. Somehow he couldn't help hoping that the two tenontosauruses had gotten away safely.

"Well, we certainly couldn't have done it without you, son," said Fenton's father, breaking into his thoughts.

"Fenton knows more about dinosaurs than anybody," said Willy, smiling at his friend.

"We certainly do owe you a big thank-you, Fenton," said Professor Martin.

"That's for sure," agreed Charlie. "You did some pretty good sleuthing on this one." He grinned. "Why, I'd say you were a regular dinosaur detective, Fenton."

They all laughed.

"Hey, Dad," said Fenton as he finished the last of his spaghetti, "what time is it?"

Fenton's father looked at his watch. "Six twenty-five."

Five minutes till Treasure Quest, thought Fenton. He looked at Willy, who was sucking up the last strand of spaghetti from his plate. Maybe Max could redesign the game a little so that three people could play.

"Willy and I will be back in a little while," said Fenton, pushing back his chair. "Come on upstairs, Willy. There's somebody I really want you to meet."

"Cool!" said Willy.

"By the way," said Lily Martin as Fenton and Willy were heading out the dining-room door, "this spaghetti sauce is marvelous."

"Thanks, Professor Martin," Fenton called back, grinning. "It's my mom's—I mean my *family's*—special recipe!"